W9-BSL-282

Anya's War

3 1526 03982159 7

Anya's War

Andrea Alban

FEIWEL and FRIENDS
New York

A Feiwel and Friends Book
An Imprint of Macmillan

ANYA'S WAR. Copyright © 2011 by Andrea Alban. All rights reserved. Distributed in Canada by H.B. Fenn and Company, Ltd. Printed in December 2010 in the United States of America by R. R. Donnelley & Sons Company, Harrisonburg, Virginia. For information, address Feiwel and Friends, 175 Fifth Avenue, New York, N.Y. 10010.

Library of Congress Cataloging-in-Publication Data

Alban, Andrea.
    Anya's war / Andrea Alban. — 1st ed.
        p. cm.
    ISBN: 978-0-312-37093-0
    1. Jews—China—Shanghai—Juvenile fiction. [1. Jews—China—
Shanghai—Fiction.   2. Emigration and immigration—Fiction.
3. Abandoned children—Fiction.   4. Sino-Japanese War, 1937–1945—
Fiction.   5. Shanghai (China)—History—20th century—Fiction.
6. China—History—1937–1945—Fiction.]   I. Title.
    PZ7.A3153An 2011
    [Fic]—dc22
                                                        2010037089

Book design by Susan Walsh

Feiwel and Friends logo designed by Filomena Tuosto

First Edition: 2011

10 9 8 7 6 5 4 3 2 1

www.feiwelandfriends.com

To attract good fortune, spend a new coin on an old friend, share an old pleasure with a new friend, and lift up the heart of a true friend by writing her name on the wings of a dragon.

—CHINESE PROVERB

Not much more than a month ago I was on the other shore of the Pacific, looking westward. This evening, I looked eastward over the Pacific. In those fast-moving days which have intervened, (the whole width of the world) has passed behind us (—except this broad ocean.)

—AMELIA EARHART

The ocean cannot be emptied with a spoon.

—YIDDISH PROVERB

prologue

*A*nya inspected the first page of her *Book of Moons* where she'd affixed the last photo Papa snapped in Odessa: of Anya shivering next to Mama and Georgi in the cold, in front of their old linden tree. Last January, she was still polite Anya of Pushkin Street, a good girl who talked a little too much but knew when to keep her mouth shut. For example, when her grandmother Babushka's dumplings weren't as delicious as their cook, Valentina's; or when the secret police was patrolling her neighborhood because spies had reported anti-Communist activity; or in case Mama was eavesdropping outside her new bedroom in Shanghai and might overhear her nightly prayer to God: *Help me tell my mother, former diva of the Odessa Opera, I am too afraid to sing onstage.*

The two black corners holding the family photo were slightly crooked, the way she had left them before her birthday lunch this afternoon. She had constructed the booby trap so if Babushka was snooping again, Anya would catch her. Babushka couldn't leave anything out of place. In her rage for order, she would have reset the corners—despite Anya's warning on page one:

To You,
who wish to spy
on my fond memories and deepest thoughts,
read at your own risk!
Anya Rosen

Papa had cut off the end of the family name when the six of them arrived at the Shanghai Custom House. "For a fresh start," he announced to Mama, who covered her face with her manicured hands. At the time, Papa hadn't admitted to her he was also changing his first name to Jake, to replace Joshua, in case Stalin's men crossed the Yellow Sea to track him down and make good on their threats. Mama refused to sign the immigration papers until Papa promised she could join the Russian Music Society, a troupe that didn't compare with the Odessa Opera but at least she would sing her favorite arias to refugee audiences. Anya's grandfather, Dedushka, didn't have to bribe Babushka. Whatever he pushed under her nose to sign, she signed . . . when it meant a speedier route to her rocking chair where she spent most of the day crocheting.

Writing outside on her terrace was how Anya prevented her brain from bursting. Once she transformed a problem into a memory, and wrote it down, she could imagine a happier outcome, especially with the river in full view. The string of white letters, like pearls on paper, represented hope. Li Mei, the family cook—who wasn't *just a servant* to Anya—hinted that the secret way to solve a problem was to think of it as a river. *Wu wei.* Let the water run its own course.

Writing was in Anya's bones. Papa was a journalist. Mama wrote invitations. Papa's father, Zayde, had long ago held the title of *shtetl* scribe of Gomel. He was the keeper of the village *Yizkor*, the Book of Memory. Zayde had inscribed the huge book with the name and job of every man in the village, and the dates of their bar mitzvahs, weddings, pilgrimages, births of each child, and eventually, their deaths. Papa agreed with Anya that the men should have remembered the women, too.

Anya dipped her fountain pen in white ink and wrote on the next black page: *July 22, 1937.* In the upper right corner, where she kept track of how many days had passed since Amelia Earhart's plane disappeared, she wrote the number: *19.* The whole world assumed the Electra plane had crashed and the first woman to fly along the equator on her journey around the world was dead. One week after the early reports, Anya asked Papa what *he* thought happened to Amelia Earhart. "You're asking me, Anush? You're the one who follows her every move."

They had been sitting on a bench in the garden as the moon rose, waiting for the summer constellations to brighten. *What if the tide carried Amelia to Phoenix Island and she is lying in the warm sand, under the same moon, stargazing. Would she be lost?* As though reading her mind, Papa said, in the same tone he used when she awoke in the middle of a nightmare, "If she can see Orion's Belt and the Little Dipper, she is fighting for her life. Where there's life, there's hope."

Anya began writing her daily entry below the date, leaving blank the customary spot to the right for her sketch of tonight's moon phase.

Today is my fourteenth birthday and my best present, besides my new bike, will be the full moon tonight, the Hungry Ghost Moon. Li Mei put moon cakes on the altar to placate the ghosts so I wouldn't have to share my chocolate birthday cake. Did you know that when you plant wishes under a full moon they have the best chance of coming true?
Here's my list:

1) *I wish President Roosevelt never calls off the search for Amelia Earhart.*
2) *I wish I could find the courage to tell Mama that I have decided: I am absolutely, one hundred percent certain that I don't want to sing opera. I think.*

It was Mama who signed Anya up with a voice coach. Mama applauded loudest at her recitals at the Odessa Conservatory and bragged that Anya was the youngest singer ever— five years old—to perform solo. Mama was desperate for Anya to sing the lead in operas internationally. Mama already had her eye on an Erté gown from the Lord & Taylor's catalog for opening night.

The gown was lovely but didn't it matter to Mama what Anya wanted?

3) *I wish my right bosom would grow extra fast and catch up with my left side so I am no longer lopsided.*

She closed her eyes and concentrated all her wishing might on number three, to the count of sixty. Then she slid her hands over her blouse. She was as flat as a moment ago, flatter than latitude. The ridge of her waist and hips were practically longitudinal.

4) *I wish a witty line to say to Bobby Sassoon will miraculously pop into my brain at bowling club on Tuesday.*

For once, could she not trip over her tongue or have trouble spitting out the words that seemed to stick behind the massive lump in her lovesick throat whenever Bobby was within earshot.

5) *I wish the Japanese would stop killing Chinese children by accident.*
Shalom,
Anya

"Peace," she said out loud, but not "amen." Babushka said "amen" at the end of *her* sentences for emphasis.

Anya and her best friend, Giselle, were convinced that when she said the word, it sounded like a curse. Babushka was a direct descendant of Baba Yaga. When an ivory figurine was nudged out of place in the curio cabinet during dusting, she exploded, double chins wagging like the Russian witch, about disorder in the house. She called Dedushka a *altekocker* if he was a mere five minutes late for *tiffin*. (Papa begged her not to call her husband an old turd at the lunch table but Babushka insisted she could call him whatever she pleased, if she said it in Yiddish.) She peered through her spectacles at Mama's and

Anya's faces, pointing out dark circles, hairs out of place, new freckles, eyeliner smudged at the edges. When Anya asked Papa why he agreed to let Mama's parents live with them in Shanghai, he explained the living arrangements were a temporary sacrifice. *He is afraid to tell Mama* nyet. *Will he ever move my cranky grandparents to their own house in Frenchtown?* Nyet.

Fortunately Babushka behaved on Shabbat, which would begin tomorrow night as soon as the sun set.

Anya adored the Sabbath, not only for the reprieve from Babushka's inspections. Magic happened on *Shabbos*, as the day of rest was pronounced in Yiddish. It was the only day of the week that was twenty-five hours long. Angels appeared, two per man, to escort him safely home from synagogue. Each Jewish person's soul was joined by a second soul. It entered the body at the instant the women kindled the Sabbath lights, then the Sabbath bride floated down from the eastern skies to dine in every Jewish home. How the bride was able to chew in millions of places at once, Anya had never figured out. Mama said it was part of the magic and be glad the Rosen family weekly Shabbat dinner was more delicious than a wedding feast.

Twenty-five hours later, when the third star twinkled in the sky, Shabbat ended with a *pfff*, the sound of the youngest child dipping the candle flame into a glass of sweet wine. On Saturday nights, Anya waited under the stars, long after her family strolled inside, for the seven Pleiades and Little Bear to appear.

In Odessa, Anya thought the stars Altair and Vega had winked at her, saying, "May you have a week of peace." But now she wondered if they had actually been warning her: Fleeing Odessa won't save your family.

The courtyard her terrace overlooked was better for echoes than her favorite catacomb in Odessa, where she spent loads of hot summer afternoons shouting at the cool walls and searching the grottos for elephant fossils.

She yelled at the side of Giselle's house next door, "Bobby. Loves. You."

"Loves. You." boomeranged on the wind current, which smelled of narcissus.

Narcissus didn't grow in Odessa but she had always wondered what it smelled like. The white flower intoxicated the gods in many of the stories Mama read to her from *Bulfinch's Mythology*. They had read their way through the one-thousand-page book— twice—on the wooden sleigh bed Mama and Papa left behind in Odessa. Well-educated children, especially those of an opera singer, were required to know the tales of Robin Hood's thievery, King Arthur's chivalry, and, of course, the misadventures of the gods and goddesses. Whenever Papa vented his disapproval of the nonsense stories, Mama had an argument ready: "How else will Anya and Georgi understand the symbolism of the arias I sing and the classical poetry they must memorize in school?" When Anya pined over the fates of Guinevere and Lancelot, Echo and Narcissus, Papa put his foot down about her flights of fancy. "Read the Talmud for how to live a productive Jewish life."

Mama always won the fight. How could you argue with this: "The purpose of literature is to amuse its readers. What is more useful than happiness?"

Only halfway through the blooming season of narcissus, Anya could well describe the aroma of the flower named after a boy who was in love with his own reflection.

It was the smell of Shanghai in July, the feeling of butterflies in her stomach when she thought of Bobby Sassoon, the taste of Li Mei's peach strudel, and Mama all dark around the eyes.

Tomorrow night, the sun would slice through gunmetal clouds above the burning *godowns*. At 7:46 p.m., the orange ball would dip below the horizon that divided her new house in the French Quarter of Shanghai from her homeland, Odessa.

Shabbat would finally begin.

Would the Japanese soldiers wait until Sunday to occupy the city?

Anya opened the *Book of Moons* again and wrote one more entry before turning in for the night:

> *Papa is sure the Japanese won't arrive until after the next ship of Jews fleeing Hitler is processed through customs. I say the sooner the better. I'm tired of the dread in this house, and the men whispering.*

Anya's War

one

Friday, July 23, 1937

Anya pedaled her new red bicycle across the thirsty lawn to save her tires from melting on the hot cement. Mama's gardeners, Yat-sen and Pearl, stopped watering the row of drooping peonies and yelled at her. By her sixth month living in Shanghai, Anya could unscramble most Chinese phrases. *Those* words were bad enough she didn't want to repeat them in her mind. She almost asked, "Didn't your mothers teach you it's rude to point a hose at Stella Rosen's daughter?" But she stopped the question from tumbling out. According to Li Mei, mosquitoes flew in and laid eggs on the tongues of foreign girls who stared at the Chinese with their lips apart.

At first, Li Mei's warnings had annoyed Anya. When Anya mumbled a derogatory comment about Babushka under her breath, Li Mei said, "A bad word whispered will echo one hundred miles." When Anya moped around the kitchen, missing Odessa, she said, "You cannot stop the birds of sadness from flying over your head, but you can prevent them from nesting in your hair."

So she imagined the day of her return to Odessa. She would drink a bottle of Coca-Cola in the shade of the linden tree where Papa took the first day of school photo every year with her oldest friends, Luba, Angelica, and Lily. Luba was oldest so she stood on the far left, then Angelica, then Lily. Anya was last because she was the youngest. When she felt lonely, she arranged the photos in a line on the dining room table, starting with *Kindergarten, 1929,* and compared where on the linden trunk the four friends' heads reached from year to year. In the last photo, *Grade 8, 1936,* Anya was four feet, ten inches tall, the shortest girl—the Jewish girl—the one unlucky enough to have a head of frizz.

*O*ver an hour ago, Li Mei gave Anya the grocery list and demanded that she *chop-chop* to Katznelson's, the kosher butcher. Tonight was meat night and Li Mei was making beef *piroshki.* Would Papa drag home a surprise guest to share the meal? Last week the Sephardic man he invited removed his sandals at the front door. Hairy-toed feet padding across her gleaming floors revolted Mama. Feet were a morbid curiosity to Anya. The only bare feet she'd seen inside Mama's house were her own flat pair. Madame Tarakanova counseled her to give up ballet; she would never get her *pointe* shoes and attain grace without proper arches.

Predicting she would have a table full to feed, Li Mei had doubled her recipe for the fried meat pies. Anya read aloud Li Mei's description of the main ingredients:

- 3 lb. beef: Ask the butcher to show you the meat before he wraps it. Check for bright red color with specks of fat. Don't let him trick you with brown meat.
- 2 medium yellow onions: Check the skin for mold.

The last items—two pomelos—were included each Friday on the list Li Mei scribbled on Mama's monogrammed stationery: no holes in the skin. Shake them good and listen for juice.

Anya knew how to choose a stupid onion, and by then, the pomelos, but she never stayed annoyed for more than a couple of seconds because, beneath the word "juice," Li Mei had drawn a cartoon picture of Anya's smiling face surrounded by a crown of curlicues.

Before Shanghai, Anya didn't know the word for the odd-looking grapefruit the size of a bowling ball. Li Mei claimed pomelo could cure her mother's bad habit of hollering and added segments to Mama's salad *daily*. Mama liked the flavor, a sweet and tart cross between strawberries and an unripe orange. Li Mei peeled a bowl full for Anya's birthday yesterday, without once squirting juice in her eyes.

But Mama hadn't smiled at the party—not even the tiniest lift of her mouth corners—when Anya puffed her cheeks like a chipmunk and blew out fifteen candles—fourteen plus one to grow on—with one big typhoon of a breath. Good girls didn't anger so she hung her head, instead of pushing her chin up and looking Mama in the eyes and admitting what was on her mind.

Will I be miserable in Shanghai on my next birthday? Will Mama ever be the mama I had B.C.?

Before China, Anya didn't try to stay out of her way. They drank darjeeling tea together in the afternoons, sitting on chairs by the window overlooking yellow, broom-covered cliffs. Georgi played in the anteroom he called Mount Olympus. He wore armor made by Vulcan, fought murderous giants and monsters with one hundred eyes, and evil dragons with his sword, Excalibur. Mama tittered when he held the wooden replica across his chest diagonally and said, "Follow me, men."

Now Mama's sad eyes stared out; eyes that were dull as a muddy pond, dark as Erebus, the place souls passed through on their way to Hell. As if she were asking, why must we mingle with Hades, when Odessa was our Heaven?

Babushka blamed Papa. He should have followed Stalin's orders that day the ugly policeman banged on the door, forced the family into the parlor, and read aloud a document, droning like a bagpipe: "You, Joshua Rosengartner, are a capitalist and therefore the enemy of Stalin and the people of Odessa. You will sign this document and join the Communist Party."

Anya hadn't understood the gravity of what he said—in the name of Stalin—until he threatened to kneel Papa down in the snow and shoot him once through his skull. When Papa shook his head *nyet*, the policeman turned on his heels, crushed the paper in his fist, and clomped out the door. Mama and Babushka staggered from the room and refused Valentina's tray of *blini* and *chai*; Papa and Dedushka cleared their throats and spit when they whispered. Instead of amen, Babushka said *oy vey* to the ceiling. Georgi drew his sword and patrolled the doors and windows while the women packed. Angry words filled the house,

4

mostly Mama's side of the arguments. ". . . Don't do this . . . my German debut . . . Joshua, no one is listening . . . I am a world-class trained soprano . . . a lifetime of voice lessons . . . No. I will not hush . . . convert . . . I don't know that God . . . Odessa is my home . . . stealing my life . . . Please join the Communists, Joshua . . . No? You won't? Ever? . . . I hate you. You are a *svolach*."

Papa-the-bastard vanished with his family like scarabs skittering under a rock, on a moonless night in three black cars, headlights off, wrapped in plaid winter coats and cashmere scarves. Mama whispered, *Lebn vi Got in Odes dos goldene land—Do svidanya.* We lived like God in Odessa, the golden land. Good-bye. The train chugged from the depot, gnashing at the rails. Mama cried like a widow. Her gloved fingers held Anya's hand, squeezing harder and harder as the train picked up speed. Mama stuffed her hands into her pockets when Odessa was gone. Anya prayed, *Send the train backward to my room and my friends.* She was afraid to reach into the darkness for Mama, and feel nothing.

If it were possible to collect her fallen tears since the last night she slept in her trundle bed, she'd have dozens of buckets to pour on the parched lawn.

two

---

*A*nya rolled across the sidewalk and off the curb with a clunk. She pedaled into the wide alley and would have flown past the Lindbergs' outdoor prep kitchen if Giselle's Number One cook hadn't whacked off the head of a huge trout. She stepped hard on the pedal brake and screeched to a stop. The tall cook, wearing a tunic stained with blood or possibly beet juice, sliced into the fish's silver belly. He boned the pink-gray flesh in one pass, and then tossed the skeleton into a wood bucket.

Poor Giselle is eating fish again for dinner. She clucked the pity sound that her friend hated. *Babushka says a girl needs one serving of meat per day in order to blush properly pink. But I adore Giselle's pearly skin.*

Giselle came to Shanghai with a mother and father, two brothers, Adam and Archibald, a sister, Leona, and their nine-month-old cousin, Davey, from Austria. And of course Davey's parents. No grandparents tagged along. They were too old to leave Berlin but weren't worried about Hitler. Promising they would stay out of trouble and shop at the groceries owned by gentiles, Giselle said Oma pleaded with her family to escape the *sturm und drang*. As long as they associated with non-Jews, the Nazis wouldn't harass them. They could make themselves scarce and avoid the growing storm and stress.

Giselle's other cook was plucking the feathers off a plump chicken. The wind, sudden as a funnel cloud, picked up the quills and scattered the pile through the air. Two boy servants poured steaming water over the slop the cooks had tossed on the ground. One of them sneered at her and pretended to throw water in her direction. *They never treat Georgi like this. But I'm a girl.* The wash water stream threatened to flood her sandals. She pulled her feet onto the pedals before the scalding stream burned her toes.

Usually she followed the bubbles, alley to alley, as they flowed into a network of gutters traversing Frenchtown. A kitten or two often joined her and pawed at fish heads and bones swirling in the whirlpools. Not today. If Anya was one minute late, Li Mei would smack her rolling pin on the wood block, spread her feet wide, jut her head, and narrow her black eyes. This transformation of her five-foot-tall, skinny body into a looming warrior had at one time elicited the fear of God in her—until it became clear that although Li Mei's voice was sharp as a crow's caw, her heart was as soft as tofu.

Although Li Mei was almost seventeen—Mama said sixteen was the official age of womanhood in China—she was just a girl in Anya's eyes. She was shorter than Anya by half a foot but seemed inches taller. Babushka said Li Mei's waist-length hair and the vertical lines of the tunics (bought for her by

Babushka so she looked presentable) created the illusion of height. Each day she wore a freshly starched top imprinted with a crane or dragon, willow tree or magpie, for nobility, good fortune, long life. Stuck through the collar was one of her lucky pins, of the Eight Immortals—the gods and goddesses who symbolized perfect happiness. These pins, and an English language dictionary, were the only possessions she carried in her knapsack when she'd moved into the Rosens' house.

Anya soared through the veil of chicken feathers with her leather camera case strapped around her neck. The bicycle tires wobbled as they clanked over uneven cobblestones. Anya gripped down hard on the handles. After her growth spurt this summer, she no longer had to stretch her arms practically out of their sockets to steer.

She had only left the house once without the Leica camera. That day last week when she forgot it on the peg in the closet, pigheaded Babushka escorted her to the parlor mirror. "Look in the mirror, so nothing awful happens to you and your family. You know it's a bad omen to return to the house for what you forgot. Amen."

Taking pictures with the Leica distracted Anya from the list of worries she wrote on the back page of her *Book of Moons*—to keep the worries separate from the wishes. The list was long right now, but after tonight, after she and Papa broke the news to Mama about singing, she'd scratch a thick white line through number two: *I hate Maestro Brodsky's breath and don't know how to break it to Mama that I'm not taking singing lessons anymore.*

If Amelia Earhart could accomplish *her* dreams—graduating

high school at sixteen, despite moving six times, flying an auto-giro across America, breaking aviation records, flying around the world—then Anya could become only the second girl in her family to attend university. Aunt Paulina was the first, and now she was a doctor. Anya planned to graduate on time from the Shanghai Jewish School, and sail for Columbia University in America.

Luba, Angelica, and Lily promised to remain loyal to their cause, too. The four girls were not going to settle for the doom of marriage at seventeen like their mothers, chasing after a brood of sticky-faced children by twenty. At least not before they explored Manhattan and the Statue of Liberty. They had signed their pledge with drops of blood from their ring fingers while reciting the Emma Lazurus poem engraved on the bronze tablet of the Statue of Liberty:

> Give me your tired, your poor,
> your huddled masses yearning to breathe free,
> the wretched refuse of the teeming shore.
> Send these, homeless, tempest-tost to me,
> I lift my lamp beside the golden door.

Sweat trailed from under Anya's straw hat to her earlobes and dripped onto her pearl earrings. On hot days, Babushka demanded she wear a pith helmet with an absorbent towel around her neck so she wouldn't develop heat rash. Babushka and Mama didn't approve of sweat. Proper young ladies perspired. But Anya wouldn't be caught dead in such an unbecoming get-up. Like

Amelia Earhart, who never wore a pilot's helmet or goggles in public, Anya wanted to be known for her sleek and feminine style.

Twelve blocks to the market and Anya hopped off her bike. She scurried from stall to stall until she found two different onion and pomelo sellers near each other. Li Mei proclaimed that competition was Rule Number One in haggling. *Now that I'm fourteen, I'm going to negotiate like the Chinese.* Sellers knew how to make extra cash on foreign girls who were shy and polite. Li Mei said, "If you don't haggle, the sellers will cheat you."

She stood in the queue to pay for the onions, and rehearsed. 1) Call out an absurdly low price. If the seller wants fifty coppers, offer five. 2) When he doesn't go for it, drop the item. He will reduce his price the farther you walk, very slowly, away. 3) Go to the next stall, and repeat, with a price that is half the previous lowest. 4) If the seller shakes his head, complain about the small size of the onion or the bruises on the bottom. Stay very calm.

"Five coppers for this moldy onion," Anya said. The words came out crackling like the dry skin of an onion.

"Crazy girl, leave my line."

The strategy wasn't working. She walked to the end of another line and once she stepped to the front, she tried the method again. The seller answered with a price, as though he was doing Anya a favor. She tossed the coppers into the jar and ran with her onions. At the pomelo stand, she dickered with the seller. Anya persuaded him to give her two for the price of one but not before his evil eye put an end to the negotiation.

Feeling gutsy now, she nabbed a sack of flour, although it

wasn't on the list. Last week, Li Mei chose the exact moment Anya found the creepy skin diseases section in Aunt Paulina's medical textbook to check the empty flour barrel in the pantry. She dragged Anya away from the page on leprosy and out from under the covers for the last-minute run to the market for another sack.

Anya flinched when the seller said, "Russian girl. Trying to Jew me down." But, voilà, she was the proud owner of a five-pound sack of flour for the price of one pound.

At the butcher shop, Anya's legs shook as she stepped through the door, one eye on her bicycle and the basket full of groceries, and the other on the cow and lamb carcasses hanging on hooks to her left. The headless animal ghosts swayed in a buzz of horseflies.

I can't breathe in here.

When she found a pocket of air that didn't reek, she sucked oxygen into her lungs. Papa admonished her the first, second, and tenth time Anya let slip to her parents that the butcher shop was spooky. "My, you are ungrateful! Where would we shop if our friends hadn't opened these businesses? Without Little Vienna, Mama wouldn't have a bakery to buy us raspberry linzer tortes. If Mrs. Podalski hadn't built Venus Café, you and Giselle would have no place to boy-watch. No Lyceum Theater, no Hollywood talkies. Mrs. Rifkin, Mr. Jedeikin, and Mrs. Podalski worked hard so you can enjoy yourself."

"And survive in this filthy town," Mama had added.

The smell of raw meat sickened Anya, as did the blood trickling into collection buckets under the metal counters. Mr. Katznelson separated and packaged meat parts while the Jewish families' cooks yelled their orders. He tossed Anya a brown package with R-O-S-E-N written on the side in chunky black letters. Holding her bare arms high so no clumps of animal fat would stick to her, she pushed through to "the Missus" collecting payments in her cash box. She was the one clean person, the other Odessan in this awful store.

Back outside, Anya crammed the meat on top of the flour sack. In case a little meat juice leaked out, it wouldn't splatter the smooth knees she'd shaved for the first time this morning.

Someone gripped and tugged her elbow with strong fingers. A mend-coat woman was inspecting the tiny hole in Anya's blouse with a monocle.

"Ouch! Let go," Anya yelled, and whirled around.

"Ugly patch better than pretty hole. I know Yiddish, Jew girl. Wantchee?" she asked, pulling colorful patches from her basket and fanning the assortment like a peacock tail.

Anya lifted her camera and focused the viewfinder on the woman's face. Old Chinese people believed that ghosts lived inside cameras and flew out to haunt anyone having their picture taken. Anya clicked the shutter again and again until the terrified woman escaped down the street.

With her basket full, Anya peddled toward home. Big Ching chimed . . . one . . . two . . . The loud sound of the clock booming the hour to all of Shanghai had bothered her when she first arrived but now she looked forward to the chime. Three . . . four . . . Anya calculated as quickly as an abacus. Five blocks home at one minute per block, enough time to detour to the harbor and take some photos before her four thirty voice lesson.

three

At the Yusen Kaisha wharf, Anya squeezed with her bike to the front of the crowd. *What is everyone pointing at?* She jostled for a better view. Yesterday, the Japanese war vessel, *Idzumo*, was anchored by itself. Now she counted six destroyers and thirteen gunboats lurking like hungry ghosts in the muddy water. She framed the shot, using the crumbling wall the Chinese built to bar Japanese pirates as the left edge, and snapped dozens of photos.

Papa promised to submit this batch to his editor at *The Shanghai Evening Post and Mercury*. Cornelius van der Starr paid more for war articles accompanied by photos. She would earn a photo credit and three coppers; one to put through the slot of the Shabbat *pushka* to send to the Zionists, one to deposit in her bank savings account, and one to fall straight to the bottom of her pocket where Papa said it would burn a hole. She was captivated by how her name looked typeset in tiny letters in a font called Bodoni running up the right edge of her photo. One of her dreams was to win a National Geographic Society Gold Medal when she was an adult.

The wind whipped the patriotic flags flying on the masts of large international ships—from England, France, and Denmark. "Red for danger and revolution, blue for perseverance, stars for the heavens, stripes for rays of the sun, and white for innocence and surrender," Papa had explained. "The flags tell the rest of the world what these countries stand for. Colors and shapes are symbols representing big ideas, the spirit of each country."

Mama planned to book passage for Anya on the *General Meigs* after her seventeenth birthday. The silvery ship would clip from the dock for the forty-mile journey down the muddy Whangpoo to the China Sea. Anya imagined her nose burning with the river's smell, and her arm, held above her head in the farewell wave of Princess Elizabeth of England. She would rotate her hand from side to side, fingers straight, her right hand in the air in line with her right ear, positioning her thumb a few millimeters forward, the tiny opalescent beads on the trim of her white gloves glittering. And Mama and Babushka would wave back, leaning toward the ship, following its wake, their fingers shaking in the wind, shoulders sagging, and teardrops falling hard on the deck. The cool sea would spray her face as she turned from the old harbor, strolled to the bow to catch the horizon on her way to college in America. She would sail to San Francisco, then ride the train to New York, watching mountains, plains, rivers, deserts, cities and towns—and Americans!—race by. Mama pretended her special request to her colleague, Apollo, wasn't utterly absurd: "Oh, god of music, I bow to you. Let Juilliard accept Anya in the opera program."

Boy, will Papa and I surprise Mama when we break the news about my real plans.

A sudden *snip-snap* like a quick whip against a horse's flank: The red danger flag slapped in the wind at the top of the weather signal tower. Anya rubbed the tears the humid wind had drawn, and stopped taking pictures.

Jules, the meteorologist from Siccawei Observatory, hoisted a single flag up the cable system. Two flags warned of a typhoon. One flag signaled a storm. A few nights ago, Li Mei predicted this rainstorm without any fancy instruments. She showed Anya and Georgi the moon through an O shape made with her thumb and index finger. "*Ta-shu* moon, means 'great heat.' But I smell rain."

"*Bonne anniversaire*, Anya," Jules said, smiling with eyes sparkling like the sky he was in charge of.

"What's the name of that new boat?" she asked.

"You mean the *Idzumo?*"

"No, the American one surrounded by tugboats."

"That's the U.S.S. *Augusta*, here from Tsingtao to protect the Americans in the International Settlement."

"I didn't believe Georgi's big news this morning. My little pygmy of a brother exaggerates every weather warning and silk farmer revolt he hears reported on the news."

"What did he forecast this time?" Jules chuckled. "Let me guess . . . a low-pressure system will upgrade into a typhoon with wind speeds of a hundred eighty kilometers per hour?"

"That's exactly what he said. How did you know?"

"Because a few days ago, while you bowled with your boyfriend, he asked me to teach him the exact terminology for describing a typhoon."

"Bobby Sassoon is not my boyfriend!" Anya reddened at the sound of her crush's name and "boyfriend" in the same sentence.

"I didn't mention any boy by name," Jules pointed out. "You just divulged your secret."

He tied a slipknot on the flag line and wiped his hands on his trousers. "Now that you're fourteen, it seems you've lost interest in my weather forecast, *non?*" He pushed his beret over his ears. "How did you celebrate your birthday yesterday?"

"Chen wouldn't drive me over here. He said the Japanese soldiers might pull him from the driver's seat and make a lesson out of him," Anya said. "I showed him a tin of lychee nuts but he wouldn't take the bribe, and Georgi threatened to tattle on me if I ditched my tea party."

"I noticed your Red Rover. The latest model . . . lucky girl." Jules winked, then his eyes became serious. "Don't blame Chen. The situation with the Japanese is very precarious. He is right to act with caution."

"Aren't you terrified up there?" She gazed at the white dome on Sheshan Hill, the largest of the buildings at Siccawei, then grabbed his arm and cried, "The Japanese are coming!"

He smoothed the top of her head, and said, "I live in the most modern lookout tower on the entire coast of China. If I spy a Japanese bomber, I promise I'll dive under my desk for cover." Jules chuckled.

"Please eat Shabbat dinner with us tonight and retell us your stories about climbing the Eiffel Tower."

"If I break for dinner, who will transmit the danger codes so ships won't crash into the coast in Georgi's typhoon?"

Anya rolled her eyes. "Please, Jules. Li Mei is making your favorite: beef *piroshki*."

"I can't. I'm sorry. *Merci beaucoup*. Next week, visit me at the observatory. I'll give you and Georgi . . . and Li Mei, a tour, and show you my methods for tracking storms."

"Can I take a picture of you demonstrating your high-powered instruments?"

"It's a deal." Jules nodded his head. "And I'll take you through Tushanwan Orphanage next door. The boys, especially the six year olds, will clamber for you to take their pictures. Now hurry home—*vite*—before the storm hits. And avoid the Wall."

Jules said *vite*. Giselle said *schneller*. Mama added *immediatement* to *vite*. *Why does everyone want me to hurry?* Anya hopped on her bike and pedaled toward the corner. She had no intention of going anywhere near the new brick and barbed wire wall built around south Frenchtown to stem the flow of refugees and protect the area from war damage.

"And send my regards to Li Mei. The most beautiful girl in Shanghai . . . in China, for that matter," he called after her.

Li Mei? Our cook? Li Mei, whose knees were knobby and whose breath smelled like garlic-flavored dragon fire?

When did Li Mei have time for a boyfriend? Did they secretly meet on her day off in the gardens of Tushanwan? She said she went home to help her mother cook the Sunday supper for the priests and orphans. Had she lied and gone on dates every week with Jules? *That's* why Jules disappeared from the Rosens' dinner table before their Friday Shabbat meal was over on the increasingly frequent occasions he joined them. One time Anya found him in the kitchen helping Li Mei set up the tea service and plate his favorite cookies—madeleines fresh from the oven—dipped in Swiss milk chocolate.

"*Oui-oui.* Yes, I will break it to Li Mei that she has a secret admirer."

"Not so secret." Jules grinned, pointing like a tour guide at Anya's neighborhood across the promenade. "Hurry!"

four

Pretending she was a gazelle, Anya pedaled home from the signal tower. Jules always said he couldn't come to dinner but would surprise them as usual and show up moments before they sat down to their meal. As Li Mei tucked sprigs of parsley garnish around the *piroshki* platter, he often popped through the kitchen door, which irritated Mama. But she forgave him because he was a Frenchman.

At the entrance to the alley, Anya rolled to the shade of the London plane trees. She pulled her blouse out from the band of her capris and waved the hem to let some air cool her sweaty skin. The crown of broad lime green leaves fanned the sidewalk. Once her face felt cooler, she pedaled toward her courtyard.

The front tire of her bicycle suddenly dipped, twisting her torso. She jerked the left handlebar to regain her balance. The heavy basket of groceries made the bike careen and fall. Anya couldn't stop the crash with her right arm. She banged her elbow and shoulder hard on the street. Her head landed on a dam of wet feathers. Loops of animal intestines bobbed by in the gutter water, and she gagged. The sack of flour had tumbled from the basket and burst wide-open with a puff, powdering the onions and two-for-the-price-of-one pomelos, which rolled away down the street.

Before Anya boarded the ship to Shanghai, Aunt Paulina had taught her a sailor's trick for quelling seasickness: *Expand your belly and lungs, then your chest, with a slow deep breath, and hold it . . . one . . . two . . . three . . . let the air push from inside out. Release.* She closed her eyes. *One. Two. Three. Four. Five.* She let her breath out through pursed lips like a whistle, inhaling and exhaling three more times.

Pulling the last feather from her curls, Anya jumped to her feet and squished the meat beneath her sandal. Bloody beef oozed from the torn package onto the dirty cobblestones. *The groceries are ruined. I am ruined. The whole neighborhood will hear Li Mei and Mama, and probably Babushka, too, yelling at me.*

Anya tilted her head to listen. *What is mewing?* No kittens were prancing around in the alley. The sound grew louder, more desperate than the stray kittens Georgi captured and held by the scruffs of their necks, then tossed into the air and caught like beanbags. It was coming from a reed basket in the gutter. She paced toward it. A bump moved across the top of the soiled burlap sack tucked over the contents. She took a step backward. Another lump poked out from the side and disappeared like a popped bubble. Anya jumped.

How silly. I am fourteen, much too old to allow a little creature to frighten me. Peek in the bag already. She tiptoed closer and lifted the basket by its handle. She plucked off the fish tail and tomato skin clinging to the bottom. Her face flushed hot.

I should go home. Now. Before Maestro Brodsky drums his fingers on the piano keyboard cover, and checks his watch.

The creature stopped moving. *Whatever is in here might fly out and bite my face.* Her heart beat like Maestro's metronome. She plopped down on the curb. She couldn't take one deep breath without gasping.

Whatever is trapped in here is alive and wants out. Shush, kitty.

In one quick pull, she lifted off the burlap. Wrapped around the kitten was a snow white cloth embroidered with a red dragon. The tassels smelled like the sandalwood incense Li Mei lit this morning to appease the Hungry Ghosts. She had caught Georgi sampling a moon cake on the offering table, and warned him of the mysterious illness he'd catch for his greed. "Don't step near the burning end of the incense stick unless you want a spirit to possess you. Where those ashes lie is an opening to the spirit world."

Anya pulled a corner of cloth the way Georgi unwrapped his birthday presents, slow as a bandage.

One tiny foot—not a paw—then another, pushed out from the swaddling. Toes—human ones—wiggled. She ripped the cloth away.

A baby girl, wearing only a yellow cap, stretched her arms and shook her head, *No, no, no.* The glint of a gold charm sewn to the side of the cap with red thread caught Anya's eye.

Anya wiped her palms on her seersucker capris and touched the baby's hair. Her locks were as dark and shiny as Papa's obsidian paperweight. *Look how beautiful her eyes are. What does she see in the sky? A Shabbat angel, perhaps?*

Her skin was the color of fresh salmon. Did she have a

disease? Thank goodness Mama had taken Georgi and her to the clinic for inoculations.

What kind of mother forgets her child in the street? Who is this baby?

The little charm jogged Anya's memory. Did she belong to the refugee wearing a moth-eaten coat slouched against their driveway column? When Anya and her family came home from Anya's birthday lunch at the Cathay Hotel, they found her fussing with a few battered pans, assorted cracked rice bowls, a porcelain teapot, and a bunch of golden trinkets scattered across her *k'ang*. Lying on the grass mat next to her thigh was a screaming infant kicking her legs in the air. The mother had pulled a droopy breast from her tattered tunic and shoved the nipple in the newborn's mouth. She had sucked and sucked like there was no tomorrow.

Anya picked up the crying baby. She nestled her in the crook of her arm as the nannies did at French Park. And she rocked the baby girl, and held her close. *Shush, shush.* Did the mother decide she couldn't feed her child and throw her away? Did she escape a village, dodging bullets, holding a cloth over her baby's face so the smoke wouldn't choke her lungs? Did she walk to Shanghai, following the curves of the Yangtze River, her happiness flowing away in rivers of milk?

Anya pushed a bent knuckle into the baby's mouth. *She's starving!* Grasping the baby's feet, Anya massaged the wrinkled soles the way Mama liked hers rubbed after a day of shopping. Anya always had trouble popping Mama's toe knuckles to straighten them so they wouldn't bend upward, as though strings were inside pulling tight. Mama's shoes, neatly lined up on the floor of her closet, had upturned toes, too.

I must be gentle with these tiny feet. Anya grazed the big toes between her fingers, feeling them grow from cold to warm.

If Mama were here, she'd hold the baby up and examine her. She'd count her ten fingers and toes. Check her hair for lice. Button her into a white lace dress. Then, she'd march to the nearest Indian Sikh—not to the Chinese authorities who might not care about a Chinese girl—report the lost child, order him to take her *immediatement* to the police station and issue an alert for the missing mother. She'd walk beside the officer, not behind him, to make sure he followed her orders exactly, *immediatement.*

"Immediately" was Mama's favorite word.

Babushka would insist this baby was none of their business. When Anya whipped her neck around to look at legs swollen black with gangrene and shivering bodies curled up in balls on the hot sidewalk, Babushka always steered her in a wide arc around them. "Bad omen to step over a whole person, or a body part. Amen."

What if the girl is sick with dysentery? What if I catch it? Diarrhea leads to dehydration. A girl can die of dehydration. Or worse, I might turn purple.

Anya's neck bristled, not from the rash. *Why did this happen to me today? I finally won my freedom. I am finally fourteen.* The gun blasts across the river had almost destroyed her plans to ride with the wind in her face, in the middle of the boulevard, hair flying behind her.

If ever there was a time to pray it was now. Dedushka had taught her that the words of her prayers crystallized her thoughts and would lead to the right action.

She pleaded out loud to her God, the One who could help her now, "God, I know I should pray to the Jade Emperor since this little girl is Chinese. Even though you are my Jewish God, could you please talk to the ruler of the Chinese heavens? Between the two of you, I'm sure you can agree to help this poor baby? Good Jews don't throw out baby girls. Mama and Papa kept *me*. The Torah says all children are precious."

All girls are precious. We're all the same.

The dark gray clouds blew together and transformed into a winged water dragon with the head of a horse, its serpentine tail waving at the city. Li Mei said dragon clouds meant "Big rain, big happiness."

"I know I've asked for too many favors lately. But isn't saving this little girl as important as finding Amelia Earhart and her plane? If you show me what to do, I promise I won't let my canaries loose in my room again. And if I do forget to latch their cage door by accident, I will wipe up the bird poop *before* Mama steps on it. Please God, give me a sign. And a new package of meat."

If Amelia Earhart were a Jewish girl, late for her voice lesson and Shabbat bath, would she postpone her dream of flying around the world—breaking a world record—for a baby thrown away by her family?

Anya scoured the ground for a flat pebble among the cobblestones and muck. She found one and brushed her thumb over the rough side, then palmed it and felt smooth, cool stone. *Let the pebble make the decision. Smooth side up, I leave her. Rough side up, I hide her in my room.*

Trying to ignore her aching knee, she took a deep breath

and tossed the pebble high into the air. She reached up to catch it, misjudging its trajectory. The pebble landed on the inner edge of a cobblestone and flipped over with the smooth side up.

Anya imagined tomorrow at dawn the sanitation workers throwing the dead infant into their wagon. Sailing through the air, limp as a rag doll, she'd land on a pile of bodies, a valley of bones nobody recognized. Next, a dead beggar, tossed like a sack of potatoes, would fall, fall, fall to rest in pieces on top of the heap.

She threw the pebble again and as it sailed up, she changed the meaning of one of the sides. *Rough side up, I search for the baby's mother.*

Anya caught it this time. With one half-opened eye, she slapped it on her palm.

The smooth side faced up. Again. The melody of a piano song floated down to where she rocked on the hard curb. Giselle was practicing the Blue Danube. *Quiet down, Giselle, I can't think.* Giselle's parents waltzed by the open window and didn't look down. Giselle's little sister, Leonie, who read poetry half the day, was probably lying on her stomach in her spot underneath the piano, chubby little legs waving in the air in time with the music.

For a few seconds more, water streamed and pooled at the curb on its gurgling way to the Whangpoo River where hungry seagulls would attack the feast of animal remains and vegetable scraps it carried. The cooks had gone inside. The alley was quiet except for the piano melody, and Archie, Giselle's brother, plucking *pizzicato* instead of bowing the violin strings, and the wind rustling the peony bushes.

The sunlight was fading. Shabbat was drawing near. Mama was interrogating Li Mei right about now: "Where in the devil is Anya?" Li Mei would hold up her I-don't-know palms. She'd refuse to admit she sent Miss Ani-ah out on her bicycle to pick up the last-minute groceries.

If I leave the baby in the gutter, she will die. If I bring her home, Dedushka and Babushka will kill me, if Mama and Papa don't get to me first.

Anya shoved the pebble in her pocket and stood up, cuddling the girl close to her heart. She walked over to the bushes and flicked the Han Xiang-Zi pendant swinging in the breeze. Giselle had bragged that two days after her mother tied the silver charm to the bottom branch it burst into bloom. Han Xiang-Zi was the happy Immortal, who made flowers bloom at will.

She plucked the widest leaves she could find, swept the cobwebs off, and made a little nest. She laid the infant down beneath Han Xiang-Zi jingling in the breeze. Li Mei believed in the magic of the Eight Immortals but Anya's parents, like most Jews, didn't. Anya was on the fence about Chinese magic. A puff of aphids rose from the ground. Anya picked a trio of the tea green insects from the baby's black hair.

"Stay right here, baby! I'm going to get Li Mei," Anya said. "Don't you worry. I'll be back in a jiffy."

Anya pulled her twisted bike from its side and nudged back the kickstand with her heel. *Poor bike. It isn't your fault I chose the shortcut home.* She hardly noticed the line of scratches on the shiny red frame.

five

$\mathcal{A}$ sudden movement in the bushes caught Anya's eye as she rolled along the alley hedgerow. *Is that a stray dog? He better not growl. That isn't a dog. It's too tall and dogs aren't yellow.* She squinted her eyes against the dipping sun. Someone was sobbing. Anya stopped.

Crashing through the bushes was a woman dressed in a yellow *qipao* hiked above her knees.

"Who are you?" Anya yelled. "Why were you hiding?"

Is she the baby's mother? She is too elegant to be a bad mother.

The woman didn't stop. Or answer. Her shoulder-length black hair shook loose from her bun and streamed behind her like kite strings. She tripped, but managed not to fall, and darted toward the corner.

"How dare you!" Anya screamed. "Please don't leave. Hey, I need to talk to you. Wait!"

Mr. Lindberg popped his head out the window. "What's the commotion? Pipe down out there . . . it's almost Shabbat."

"It's me, Mr. Lindberg. Anya," she said, trying to make her voice sound calm and confident.

"Anya? What trouble are you in now?"

Mr. Lindberg always looked on the negative side of a situation. Giselle said he was impossible to live with since the Nuremburg Laws prevented him from working in Berlin's banking industry and the Nazis had forced him to sell his bank to a German who wasn't Jewish.

"Georgi's ball. It rolled in here. Sorry to bother you right before Shabbat, Mr. Lindberg."

Thank God the sun hasn't gone down yet. Lying on Shabbat was the worst sin.

"Please tell Giselle she is invited for breakfast after we walk the birds tomorrow."

"Enjoy your *Shabbos*, Anya Rosen."

Pull your head in. Now. Please.

Anya jumped off the bicycle and lifted the kicking baby from under the shrub. She put her into the bicycle basket, and charged toward the corner, talking to the baby as she pedaled furiously. "No matter what, I won't let you die. I will catch your crazy mother. I don't care if I'm late for the beginning of Shabbat and Mama sends me to my room without *piroshki*. I will find your mother."

At the corner, she knew exactly how to avoid getting trampled by the crowd. The first time a swarm of Chinese people had swept her up—so different from Odessan crowds—she felt helpless. But she quickly learned how to move with the flow, like a fish in the river. Anya steadied her bike, and as she rolled along, spun her head in three directions. The woman in yellow shouldn't be too hard to spot in a sea of gray tunics.

About a hundred yards down the block, Anya saw the woman had stepped onto the Jiu qu Qiao, the Bridge of Nine Turns, and was beginning to zigzag across.

"Trip her! Stop her!" Anya shouted, and waved her arms, but drums and bells, hoots and the wind muffled her pleas.

She raced to the bridge entrance and screeched to a stop. The baby's eyes crushed shut and she whimpered. *How will I protect my new bike?* A thief would wait until she turned her back and swipe her Rover. *Catching that woman is more important than my bike.* She pulled the infant out of the basket.

Her scarf lifted from its loose grip around her tiny shoulders and floated on an updraft. Anya reached to snag it but it sailed onto the high branch of a jacaranda tree. She sprinted through the first turn of the bridge, and then the next. Each twist was a coil of a dragon tail, according to Georgi, who had explained the clever reason for the bridge's odd construction. He said evil spirits could only chase their prey in a straight line and were unable to navigate the nine corners. That bridge protected the customers of the Huxinting Tea House on the other end.

The baby's quiet cries turned into wailing. *I hope no one thinks I'm kidnapping her!*

On the ship to Shanghai, she had worried that pirates would drug and *shanghai* Papa and Georgi to serve as slaves on their clipper ship. "Instead of imagining the worst," Papa had said, "think of the other meaning of shanghai: 'city above the sea.'"

Anya burst through the strings of wooden beads in the

doorway of the teahouse. One strand hit her nose and made her right eye water. The hostess appeared from the shadows. She shushed Anya and placed her hands on her shoulders, turned her around and shoved her out the door.

"This is a quiet teahouse. No babies allowed."

"The lady wearing a yellow dress . . . I need to speak to her. It's urgent. Where is she sitting?"

"No yellow dress in there. The nobility don't patronize my lowly teahouse. I am not a member of their social class."

"I'm not interested in the whereabouts of a noblewoman. Just a young woman wearing yellow."

"The police will jail your friend as a rebel for wearing yellow unless she is gentry. Maybe you are color-blind?"

"She is definitely not noble," Anya said under her breath.

"Sorry, no one is here today. See?" She pointed to the empty tables and overturned chairs. "The Japanese are coming. Everyone is afraid. Go home, little girl, before the wind blows you and your baby away."

"I am fourteen," Anya said, and pulled herself up to look taller than five feet, two inches.

"Why would a noble mother leave her ugly baby in the care of a foreign girl?"

"She isn't ugly. She is adorable."

The proprietress scowled. "You know nothing about us! We pretend our babies are hard on the eyes so hungry ghosts will pass by our houses and instead snatch pretty foreign babies. My four-month-old boy is taking his nap and I want him to keep his soul. Leave."

You are as mean as Baba Yaga. Anya's hand reacted, instead

30

of her voice, and she couldn't control the urge to destroy something. She grabbed one of the bead strands and pulled hard. The string snapped, sending wooden beads clicking across the deck slats and dripping into the lotus pond where they sank through ribbons of algae and minnows.

Big Ching rang five times. *Oh my God, bean cakes.* It was time for Jun, the bean cake man, to arrive with Shing, the traveling tinker. Anya and Li Mei waited together six days a week for Jun's *tock-tock* and Shing's *ching-chink* accompaniment. They sold their wares in the Jewish section of Frenchtown every day except for Saturday when *halakah* forbade Jews from handling money.

Anya clutched the baby close and ran along the eight turns back to her bike, which, thank God, was where she had leaned it. She nested the baby in her basket. As she straddled the seat, she looked at the teahouse door, willing the woman in yellow to walk through the bead curtain, her arms outstretched for the baby, saying, "Thank you, young lady, for saving my daughter. It is my pleasure to reward you for your courage and honesty."

Before she noticed her tires were rolling, she brushed the shin of a teenage girl who was setting down her grandfather from his piggyback ride. The girl peeled his leathery arms from around her neck and curled over to rub her leg. The man's head bobbled like Dedushka's.

"I'm so sorry," Anya said, and steadied the old man.

The girl sneered at Anya and pushed her hand away. She grabbed Anya's handlebars and shook the bike as if she were shaking an enemy. A stream of angry words rifled through her missing front teeth. Her eyes were glued to the bicycle. Anya

31

deciphered a few phrases from the mostly unrecognizable Chinese dialect, ". . . you rich girl . . . so powerful. I will go faster . . . your bicycle . . . mine, okay?"

Tiny bumps prickled up Anya's spine. "Stop! Step away from my bicycle."

The girl batted away flies from her grandfather's face. He shot Anya a warning look. "Run like the dickens at the sight of an evil eye or you will lose your memory," Papa often warned Georgi so he wouldn't fall into the trap. The urge to push the girl was strong, to push her away hard. Anya's hand tingled the same way it had when she grabbed for the beads. That's what boys did when they hated each other. Girls kept their fists to themselves. Kept quiet. Good girls.

Anya bent her arm back to punch but she pushed the thief instead. *Crick-crack.* The girl's ribs floated away from Anya's palm.

Mortified, she jumped on her bike seat and rode away like a racer, leaving the girl gasping like a catfish.

It was only half a block before she felt terribly guilty. She had stopped the thief and defended her property, but she wasn't happy that she had hurt her. She felt ashamed. *I should go back and apologize. But I can't face the evil eye. I will not lose my Odessa memories.*

What is the fastest route home? Certainly not busy Boulevard Edward VII, the street that divided the French Concession from the International Settlement. Giselle said Adam knew all the shortcuts between the main roads. He traveled through the narrow *lilong* to get wherever he was going fast. But men smoked opium in the doorways, and thugs were waiting in dark corners to kidnap little girls. *Are these dangers Mama describes real?* The houses were squeezed together, with outer doors leading inside to courtyards and another row of houses. Who knew what lurked in the hidden spaces?

She stopped at the entrance to a lane that appeared to head north but could have headed east or west for all she knew. *Which one lets out at my street?* Eventually she would exit at the other end and arrive *somewhere.* "You only go halfway into the darkest forest before you come out the other side," according to Li Mei. The sun glinted on the copper drainpipes of the skinny three-story brick houses. Magenta, turquoise, and red underwear fluttered on metal rods stretched from each second-floor window like saluting arms. The air was purple with dusk and smelled like steam and rose soap.

Stools, buckets, and pottery covered the cement stoops. No one bothered to sweep Shanghai's messy walkways, but these front stoops were as clean and welcoming as the entrance to Anya's house. Children and dogs who didn't seem to belong to anyone in particular ran up and down the steps. On the wall next to each door there was an address made of iron numbers and a rectangular box with a little hinged door.

The baby hadn't stopped fidgeting since the bridge. *Is it my imagination or is she shriveling up?* A woman scrubbing laundry stared at Anya; actually, at the baby. Were her eyes wicked, or merely curious? *She doesn't know I hurt that skinny girl.* Anya considered confessing her crime to the laundry lady. Or reminding her that Mama said staring is impolite, even though Madame Chiang Kai-shek, the wife of the man in charge of China, stared, too.

33

The boxes can't be for mail. There aren't any slits. One of the box doors was ajar. Inside the nook, condensation glistened on a glass milk bottle. *Thank you, God, for snapping your fingers and providing one full bottle! This one time, do you mind if I break your law: Thou shalt not steal?* Fresh milk would save the baby's life. If she didn't borrow a bit, the law she might break—Thou shalt not murder—was much more serious. Anya peeled off the paper cap and smelled, then dipped her finger in the milk. It tasted sweet. How was she going to pour the liquid into the baby's mouth?

She will starve to death if I don't feed her now.

Anya folded the paper into a scoop, poured in some milk, and tipped it into the tiny mouth. The baby swallowed and opened her lips for more. Some of the milk sputtered out but in Anya's next attempt, all the liquid remained in her mouth.

From above her head, Anya heard *Tsk, tsk.* Next to the woman on the balcony, a black poodle whirled in circles, yip-yapping around a large porcelain pot planted with a miniature lemon tree. *Oh no! Not another evil eye.* Three more women fanning themselves on three neighboring balconies spoke to her in sharp tongues.

"Sit down and play with me. That will shut them up," a Chinese girl approximately Georgi's age said. She was stretched out on the stoop on her stomach, glaring at a game board. Along the other edge, a small turtle walked, occasionally venturing onto the board without knocking over the wooden playing pieces.

"I don't have time to play silly games," Anya said. She affixed the cap on the bottle and nudged it into the basket next to the baby's feet, hoping the cold glass wouldn't upset her.

"Xiang Qi requires great strategy. It's not silly!" the girl said, and cupped her chin in her hands, then moved a black etched piece to its next position. "That isn't your daughter."

"Do I look old enough to be a mother?" Anya said.

"No, and you also don't look Chinese enough to have a Chinese baby. You're a good fortune white girl."

"I found her on the street behind my house and I'm trying to catch her mother."

"Why didn't you leave her there with the others?"

Anya's chest felt tight. Her legs were leaden and didn't want to move. *I might as well fall down on the steps of this stoop.* "I can't bring her home and I'm not going to put her back in the gutter!"

"Around the corner, there's a foundling home. Look for the purple door."

The girl hopped to the other side of the board, and lifted the turtle, placing him across from her.

I don't have time for another detour! I've missed piano, the groceries are late, and Mama—oh God, Mama!

Anya pushed her bicycle through the hordes of people coming home for supper. She followed the shrieking wind to the corner. Ringing bells swung from upturned eaves that were green as moss, or a turtle shell.

The brightly colored door of the foundling home was exactly where the girl said it would be. Anya lifted the sleeping baby from the basket and twisted the doorbell. When no one answered, she banged urgently on the wood door. A young nurse wearing a navy blue uniform answered, and without asking what Anya wanted, showed her where to park her bike and ushered her across the courtyard. *Scritch-scritch-scritch* echoed from the walls. They headed toward a door with the symbol of a stork above its frame, passing a barefoot man bent at the waist, his hand resting on the small of his back. He swept the flagstones with a spindly twig broom and scurried after the occasional leaf that spiraled down from the branches of an old tree. His tattered shirt was as brown as the riverbanks. Anya hoped the orphanage wasn't dirty, too.

"Hurry up, bring her inside before my shift ends," the nurse said. She yanked Anya's waistband.

"Let go of me!"

I am not going through that door until I give the baby a name.

None of her favorite girl names fit. She wasn't a Rachel. Or a Natasha. Pearl was closer. Then the perfect name appeared in her mind.

Anya whispered "Kisa" into the baby's pink ear. "Kisa is Russian for 'pussycat.' Shalom, Kisa."

The orphanage smelled like Georgi's bathroom, and worse than Mr. Katznelson's butcher shop. Flies and gnats buzzed and lit on her face and arms. Anya pressed her hand against her eyes and followed the nurse through the frenzy of insects.

"You are not Chinese?" said the nurse, as if she wasn't sure.

"But Kisa is. Will you keep her until I locate her mother?"

"This is a home for foundlings. If you know she has a mother, then why are you here?"

"Because she's lost!"

"What is your name?"

"Someone abandoned her behind my house in Frenchtown." Anya quelled her impatience. "My name is Anya. I am too young to take care of a baby. But I can't let her die."

With that, Anya sat down on the cold floor in the middle of a room crowded with dresser drawers and old baskets filled with howling, cooing, snorting, and babbling babies. The smell and noise blasted her nose and ears, even her eyes. She could almost taste the mildew.

The nurse frowned and lifted Kisa from Anya's arms. "You live in the French Quarter? You are a Jew?"

"Yes. Does that matter?" Anya picked herself up.

"*YouTaNin, Ho*," she said. "Jews are very good, and rich, too. The mother found you on purpose."

"I don't understand."

"Most girls are unwanted and are drowned in the river."

Anya winced at the image of infants sinking to their deaths.

The nurse shuffled between the makeshift beds. *Is that a rat's tail weaving between the drawers?* As the babies exercised their legs and arms and tried to roll over, the makeshift cradles creaked and moaned. In the other half of the room, four nurses tended babies in shiny red enamel cribs.

"Are those babies sick?"

"Naive girl." She shook her head. "Those have the best chance of finding homes. They are strong and healthy boys. Sturdy boys are necessary. Girls are worthless."

Anya gulped and shook her head.

The nurse pointed to a salmon-colored patch on the back of Kisa's neck. "A stork bite. This is a good omen."

"Does that mean you'll find her a family?"

"She is not sick?"

"No. Just hungry. I fed her a bit of milk a few minutes ago."

"No more milk. She will sink into sleep faster." The nurse

laid Kisa down in a drawer and covered her with a cloth. "Don't worry. She will die in a warm room, not outside with the animals. We will make sure she is buried in a grave."

Anya's brain would explode if she heard one more word. Now she understood. The ghosts were hovering ready to snatch the girls when they fell into their final sleep, dead from dehydration, on purpose.

The smell Anya couldn't place before was death. *This is a dying room.*

To save her son from Pharaoh, the mother of Moses lined a papyrus basket with tar and pitch and dropped him in the Nile, hoping he would float to safety.

Aunt Paulina, a doctor, would not leave Kisa here to die.

Amelia Earhart would not have given up the chase for a woman running away from her child.

Anya whisked Kisa from the splintery drawer and, faster than Achilles, leaped from the room, out the door, past the sweeping man. He tossed the leaves in his dustpan into the air. Floating with pieces of a nest and jagged shell chips of a broken egg, the leaves landed a few at a time on the pavement beside Anya's front tire. Anya scooped up four and lay them, then Kisa, next to the bottle of milk in her bicycle basket, careful not to scratch the baby's face.

"You're coming home with me where I'll keep you safe," Anya whispered.

The old man pointed up through the branches and clung to the tree's trunk, then dropped his head into a cradle he made with his bony bent elbows. "Planes. Hear them?"

Wind sung in the tree and newly fallen leaves skipped across the courtyard. Children wailed. A flock of swallows lifted out of the leaf cover, then settled back into the crown of the branches. *Swallows always come back home.* No motors. Not a gun or bomb blast now. The war had grown quiet for dinnertime?

Knock. Knock. Knock. The sweeping man tapped his forehead against the thick, knotted trunk of the gingko tree, as Anya rolled her bike out through the purple door.

Lulled by billows of wind, Kisa fell asleep before Anya arrived at the last curve of her winding driveway. She leaned her bike against the lattice and lifted the baby out of the basket. She plucked a sprig of jasmine and tucked it into Kisa's wrap.

"Welcome to the Rosens!" Anya touched her cheek. *Good, she is warm and breathing.* "Stay asleep, Kisa, and we won't get caught."

six

Holding Kisa close to her pounding chest, Anya snuck in the front door. She whispered a wish to save her backside. "May Li Mei not notice I destroyed the groceries and brought home a baby. Amen." Maestro Brodsky was long gone. He waited a mere five minutes for tardy students and it was now a whole hour past four thirty.

No one else was dallying in the parlor. She rushed down the hall, and did not stomp as was her habit. She stepped around the seven squeaky spots on the polished floors. In a stroke of bad luck, she scuffed the wood with her sandal and almost tripped. Dedushka, who always walked with his bobbling head down, possessed the magical ability to identify whose shoes caused marks and expected the rulebreaker to fall to his or her knees (usually hers) and buff with spit and a rag until the dark oak floor shone again.

Anya didn't stop to wipe away the scuff. She darted past the kitchen door. But when she heard Li Mei calling out *laowai!* as an accusation instead of a respectful hello, she retraced her steps. This was not a good sign. Li Mei's voice was full of fire.

"Pay two piece. Bym-bye makee pay," she said in pidgin, to Jun and Shing, scolding the two sellers.

Jun bowed to Li Mei. "Yes, you may pay later. So sorry we are late." With fingers flying like hummingbird wings, he chose two flat flour cakes from his basket and slipped them into a container of bubbling peanut oil hanging from a shoulder pole. "Street fighting blocked our way here."

Anya salivated. The smell of browning cakes teased her nostrils. She almost forgot her mission to sneak to her room undiscovered. Jun fished the cakes from the oil, dabbed each with red paste, placed one on a piece of waxed paper, and put the packet in Li Mei's palm.

"For Miss Ani-ah," he said, holding out the other packet.

"Maskee, never mind," Li Mei said, and stuffed Anya's cake in her mouth. "Late girls don't eat."

Anya almost screamed *no fair!* both at her growling stomach and her growling cook. *Because I peeked inside a basket in the gutter, I won't eat the bean cake made especially for me.* Anya sniffed the fried cake aroma in the air. *Saving Kisa is more important than filling my belly.*

She climbed the stairs by twos, trying not to jiggle the baby. Before the hallway jutted right, she stopped and peeked around the corner. Her heart banged harder than a hammer. None of the servants were polishing brass doorknobs or unfurling the rugs Georgi rolled this morning so he could skate the hall in his stocking feet.

She ducked into her bedroom undetected. Amelia and Pidge fluttered in unison when the door opened. *Shush. Shush. Shush,* she warned her canaries. She stuck her head into the hallway one more time before she nudged the door shut with her scraped knee. The birds cocked their heads, startled, as though she was a ghost.

"Georgi will know I'm home if you don't shut your mouths," Anya whispered.

She dug into her pocket for a carrot from her stash of bird snacks, generally raw vegetable scraps from the outdoor prep kitchen or cashews from the teak bowl on Dedushka's nightstand. The blare of Georgi's short wave radio seeped through the wall separating their bedrooms. Was the announcer reporting good news for once? *Amelia Earhart is alive. The Japanese are retreating. No one hates the Jews anymore; you can go back home.* Instead, electric static and garble blasted from the speaker.

Kisa's eyes fluttered open. Her mouth scrunched in pain as though a bee had stung her cheeks.

"Don't make noise now, little one," Anya whispered, and held her up to the birdcage to distract her. "Kisa, meet my canary girls, Amelia and Pidge. I named them for Amelia Earhart and her little sister. I like the way Pidge sounds. Say it one hundred times. Pidge. Pidge. The sound tickles your tongue."

Pidge sang with her beak closed, a beautiful hollow bell sound. Anya wished Amelia sang, too, instead of chirping like a chicken. "Amelia Earhart is lost like you, Kisa."

Kisa jerked her arms. Amelia eyed her and flapped her

wings. A fluff of lime feathers floated through the bars, landing on Kisa's lips.

"It's OK, Amelia, Kisa won't hurt you," Anya said, cooing to calm the bird and reassure the sneezing baby, and herself. She lay Kisa on her coverlet and smoothed her ratty hair.

An imaginary dwarf inside Anya's skull beat her brains with a wooden fish. *Oh my God, I brought a throwaway into Mama's house! How am I going to care for a baby when I just learned how to braid my own hair?* Kisa purred and stretched her legs. Anya inspected a jagged stump on her belly, blood flecked, wrapped with red thread. *This is how belly buttons look at birth! Will it eventually fall off, leaving a perfect little cave for lint?*

After changing into her silk robe, Anya lay down. Sweat dripped down the back of her neck. There wasn't a single comfortable spot on the bed. Her mouth watered with images of butter melting on warm challah, and cinnamon steam puffing from the three holes she made with her fork tines in her slice of apple strudel. Thoughts of food jumbled together like the foamy yolks and whites Li Mei whisked in her copper bowl for Papa's breakfast eggs.

Thump. Thump. The noise came from outside on the terrace. She bolted up and looked through the glass of the terrace door to see if Georgi was spying on her again. One of the bamboo screens had fallen over. *Phew. All clear.* Chen would secure it with rope later.

From under the mattress, Anya pulled her *Book of Moons*. *Check.* The corners were still offcenter. *Check.* No smell of garlic. She fished her pen and bottle of ink from the drawer and sat at her desk.

Dear Not-Noble Lady:

I searched my neighborhood for you today. You sure run fast for a girl.

When you return for Kisa, you can name her whatever you want.

But I've given her a Russian name that means "cat." That's what she sounded like when I found her in the alley, mewling, hungry, dirty, overheated, tantalizing prey for a dog, abandoned by her mother. (Yes, you should feel guilty.) I'll take care of her tonight but I can't give her a home forever. I'm only fourteen. "Oy vey" is what my Babushka will say if she catches me hiding a baby in my dresser drawer. Please collect your daughter immediatement. (That means immediately in French.)

Sincerely,
Anya Rosen

If Anya was a magician, she'd discover Kisa's address and she'd march there and she'd bark, "I found your little girl. Take care of her like a good mother should." And then she'd place Kisa in her real mother's arms and warn the father not to argue with her.

Kisa cooed like a mourning dove in her sleep. *Is she dreaming of her mother?*

Anya tiptoed to the French doors leading out to the terrace, the one place in Shanghai she forgot her problems and made plans for her future. How was she going to tell Mama about college in America, a liberal arts education not music school, possibly followed by medical school like Aunt Paulina, her dream of finding an art colony near Columbia where she could learn the technique for developing and printing her own photos, where she could be the real Anya, who preferred singing songs to Bobby Sassoon in her marble bathtub, not singing arias on stages across France, England, and Italy. *Is Amelia Earhart floating in her lifeboat, lost and cold in the ocean? Does she have a jug of fresh water to drink and food rations? If she can survive circling sharks, then I'd better be courageous, too.*

"Don't be scared. It's me," a voice from the garden below her said.

"Giselle!" She was relieved to see her. "*Shush.*" Anya pointed to Georgi's room, an ominous look on her face as her friend climbed the lattice. Giselle always avoided the front door to avoid Babushka.

"What's wrong?" Giselle threw her leg over the railing. "I had that feeling I get whenever you're in trouble."

"Can you keep my biggest secret ever?" Anya said, picking leaves from the part in Giselle's hair.

"Who saved the day when you snuck out to the bowling alley? Your mother reminded me twice what would happen if you smashed your piano fingers in a bowling ball," she said, mimicking the snap sound.

"Quiet. Georgi is listening." Anya mimed Georgi's cheek pressed flat against the wall.

Kisa's urgent cry from the bedroom and a round of gunfire across the river stopped their banter.

"You were wondering about my secret?" Anya sprinted into the room, followed closely by Giselle. Kisa was wailing. "Georgi will tell Mama. Help me calm her down!"

45

Giselle picked Kisa up, swaying from one foot to the other. "Anya Rosen, what in the name of Sarah, Rebecca, Rachel, and Leah?"

For the first time, Anya wished Georgi would wind the volume on his radio to the loudest setting. Kisa stopped howling and sucked on Giselle's knuckle.

"I fed her a tiny bit of milk before I took her to the Foundling Home. *After* I found her lying in the alley gutter in a basket! Have you been inside that awful slimy place in the *lilong*? Girls die there—"

"Poor thing," Giselle said, and stroked the pointy mountain peak of Kisa's head. "Why did you pick up *this* baby? We've seen so many others and walked right by."

"I don't know why! I just did. It was *bashert*. Can you borrow some bottles and diapers from Davey?" Anya begged. "Please."

"Don't you have goat's milk? That's what Aunt Hannah feeds Davey."

"Ew. Goat's milk tastes so—"

"Goat-like?"

Anya giggled. "Yes, exactly."

"You can't hide her from Li Mei. She can smell a lie."

"I haven't lied to her yet."

Anya nested the baby in the pillow cradle. She hiccuped and waved her fingers like sea oats on a windy day. The sides of her mouth shaped into a crescent moon and she passed a puff of gas. Giselle fluffed the pillows and added one more to make a taller wall.

Was telling Li Mei a good idea? *Li Mei is Mama's servant and I am Mama's daughter so by deduction Li Mei is my servant, too.*

46

"Stay here and watch her while I go to the kitchen, will you, Giselle?" It was more of an order than a request. She had to practice her you-are-my-servant voice.

Dandan, the amah who cleaned their house and ironed laundry, was whistling a melody while washing dishes that Anya had not heard before. Her back was turned to the icebox. Mochou was mashing with the force of her whole body the lumps out of boiled potatoes. Li Mei wasn't in the kitchen cooking. *She's looking for me, and the groceries. I bet she's furious!*

Anya's plan to fill a glass with milk from the icebox—she assumed a cow was as good as a goat in a pinch—and to take the miniature spoon from the crystal salt dish wasn't going to work. Too many servants around.

She thought of the bottle of milk from the *lilong* she had left in her basket. Maybe it was still safe to drink.

Fortunately, Chen hadn't moved her bike into its parking place in the garage. The bottle wasn't cold to the touch anymore but she sniffed the milk and it wasn't sour. She raced inside with it and up the stairs back to her bedroom.

The pillows had fallen over on top of Kisa. *Giselle is shirking her duty.* When Anya uncovered Kisa, she was flushed purple like a concord grape, and screaming like a banshee.

"Giselle?" Anya looked in her closet, then out on the terrace. No one. *Thanks. Some friend you are.* She checked the lattice next. Papa would say, "Give Giselle the benefit of the doubt."

Anya scooted close to Kisa on the soft mattress. It buckled under her weight and she fell over, spilling milk on her yellow plaid coverlet. How was she supposed to pour milk *into* Kisa's mouth when she couldn't balance?

"Open up, little complainer."

Anya poured a little milk directly onto the baby's tongue. She swallowed most of it except for the few drops that trickled from the corner of her mouth.

"I like milk, too. May I have a sip?" Anya asked. "Georgi won't share his milk with me. Will you, little sister?"

After feeding, Kisa's eyes closed and her head dropped. Anya felt sleepy, too. Did she have time to nap before the candle lighting? Her clock read 6:20. No time to rest. How would she manage all these hungry mouths: her birds', this baby's. Her own.

Anya heard a loud bang on the terrace. *Giselle is back!* Now Anya would ask Giselle how to put a nappy on Kisa. She glanced to see if Kisa was still sleeping and then pulled up hard on the doorknob—Papa's trick for days when the moist heat swelled the wood—in order to get the door to budge. She tripped outside.

"Come and look at how cute Kisa is when she's sleeping," Anya said to thin air.

Georgi's door, not Giselle landing on the deck, was the noisemaker. It was flapping and hitting the bamboo. *Bad boy Georgi forgets to push the button on the lock and he never gets in trouble for it.*

Anya entered his room. "I'm not playing hide-and-seek. I know you're in here."

She hunted in the dust bowl behind his desk. No Georgi. He wasn't under the messy bed. *How does he get away with not making it?* Babushka inspected her bed for tidy hospital corners and forced her to pick each piece of lint from the forest green rug. Next, Anya walked into the hurricane closet. Toy soldiers and figurines of the Eight Immortals positioned for action spilled out. An army of Lu Dong-Bins wearing magic swords in back slings, on top of miniature tanks, peeked out from stacks of rocks Georgi had carted in from Soochow Creek, ready to slay dragons and conquer the Japanese. He had set up a barracks in Anya's discarded dollhouse. In the kitchen of the dollhouse, He Xian-Gu, the woman Immortal who Lu Dong-Bin was said to have rescued from a demon, was cooking sesame seeds for the men.

How come Babushka doesn't come in here, too? Mama takes away my privileges when Babushka complains about my room, never Georgi's.

Anya didn't waste any more time looking for her brother, who must have snuck downstairs to the kitchen for a snack.

Out on the terrace, she tripped over toes in a sandal. Georgi jumped from behind the screen with his arms bent like a ghoul. "I heard the *kisa* in your room? How did you sneak it in? That cat will tear the wings off your birds."

"Pipe down, pest. Your *voice* could kill a canary." *Let Georgi think Kisa is a cat.*

Anya grabbed his elbow and yanked him toward his room, but he struggled from her grip, darted into her room, and dropped to his knees, crawling like a weasel. Before she could stop him, he lifted her dust ruffle and looked underneath her bed at her collection of dried apple cores. That was one place Babushka never bothered to inspect because once she bent over, she couldn't straighten back up.

Anya scooped Kisa off the mattress to protect her from the rough boy. A disgusting, sticky, gooey, warm, wet glob leaked from her wrap and dripped on Anya's coverlet. It was black, tinged with green, and smelled sour and sweet like Amelia's and Pidge's poop.

"Oh, for creep's sake, Kisa. What a mess!" Anya cried.

Georgi jumped to his feet, holding a toy soldier he'd retrieved from one of his secret war scenes. His eyes popped wide open. Not a word came from his gaping mouth.

"What are you? Mute? It's not polite to stare," Anya said.

"That is no cat," Georgi cried. "Are you nuts?"

"No one wants her. I couldn't leave her alone in the gutter."

Anya put Kisa on the bed and released a sigh from her puffed-up chest. "Do you close your eyes when you're outside? Does Mama cover your precious face when you pass people dying on the streets? If I hadn't brought her home—"

"—I bet a thief kidnapped her and her parents are running through the alleys of Shanghai searching for her," Georgi said.

Anya clenched her fist and pounded her pillow as she imagined nipping flies swirling Kisa's face, a man dropping her body in an unmarked pauper's grave. No one to fly a silk kite in her memory, letting the string out farther and higher, then cutting it so the kite could rise up and greet her soul.

Georgi's face twitched. He wrapped his arms around Anya's waist. "Annie, please don't have a fit."

"Canaries are what I know, not babies," she said. *Why does Kisa cry so much? Is she thinking, Feed me, I'm starving. Hold me, I'm alone?*

She swept her brother's stubby crown where thick curls once grew. When he was one, he followed her around the apartment with his plump arms outstretched to her. When his legs grew sturdy enough to carry him into the garden, he held on to the edge of the mosaic birdbath, whistling and imitating the calls of warblers and tanagers.

"What will we do?" Georgi whispered.

"We both need to calm—oh, no!"

Kisa screeched. Pidge had escaped from her cage in a flurry of feathers and was perched on Kisa's face. The baby's cheeks turned a shade of scarlet. She jerked her legs and arms. The room filled with her cries, the canaries' shrieks, and Anya yelling at herself, "You idiot! You numbskull!"

"You're the stupidest mother ever," Georgi said.

"It's *most stupid,* not *stupidest,*" Anya hissed. "Close the door to the bathroom!"

She yelled the warning too late. Pidge had already flown into their shared bathroom and perched on the edge of the toilet seat.

"I will flush Pidge out to sea if you don't let me hold Kisa." Georgi pretended to flick at the bird and yank the flush chain.

"Stop!"

Georgi scooped Kisa into his arms. "Most stupidest," he said, and scooted into the bathroom and slid into the tub. Pidge flapped in circles above Georgi's head.

"You better obey your sister." Giselle ran in from the terrace and dropped a pile of diapers, safety pins, soft rags, and assorted layette on Anya's dresser.

"*Fra diavolo.* Give her to me." Anya strained for the bundle Georgi held in his lap.

"I'm not a little devil. Go eat a poison apple, and die, Snow White."

"Be quiet, *moguchaya kuchka*. I don't want the whole wide world to find out."

"Mogu—what was that?" Giselle giggled.

"*Moguchaya kuchka*. It means 'mighty handful.' Perfect nickname for my naughty brother."

Pidge fluttered her wings as she chewed on Anya's lamp cord.

"Give Kisa back or I will sic Pidge on your radio wires."

"Let me out of the tub without a scratch, I give you the baby. Touch me and I turn the water on."

"Give him space to climb out." Giselle pulled Anya's hand and they sat down next to each other on her bed.

Georgi got out of the tub when he was good and ready. He walked toward the girls with his arms outstretched, offering Kisa to them. Anya gave him the good-boy nod and reached for Kisa, but before she got hold of her, Georgi snickered and dashed from the room.

"Li Mei!" Georgi called down the stairwell. "I need you, now!" His voice screeched like rusty trolley wheels.

Anya and Giselle chased him down to the kitchen.

Before they closed in on him, he practically threw Kisa into stunned Li Mei's arms, turned around, and tugged Anya's robe sash. It loosened and ballooned and lifted behind her as though two royal attendants were holding it up like a train.

"I hate you," Anya screamed, fumbling to pull the fabric around her body. Had Pidge not been on the verge of sailing out the window, she would have slapped Georgi's cheek.

"The ceiling fan. Giselle, catch Pidge!" Anya yelled.

The fan was about to paddle the canary to death. Giselle

seized her tail feathers, and cupped her in her hands. Pidge settled into the safe, dark cave.

"Anya's trying to kill us with a stray baby she calls a cat," Georgi said.

"Your mama will not appreciate the ruckus you three are making. She is in no condition to deal with your antics." Li Mei glared. "Who is this?"

"Babushka is afraid we will catch cholera from poor people walking down the street," Georgi said. "Imagine what we could catch from a gutter baby."

"Shut up. She's not sick," Anya said.

Kisa drooled foamy milk, splattering Li Mei's shoulder, and mewing rhythmically.

"And you, dawdling Anya. Where are my groceries?"

"Is a spotless onion more important than an infant? You made me chop-chop to the market and I was in such a hurry to get home that I fell off my bike and practically landed on top of her by the side of the curb."

"Ai-yah! Where is my meat?"

"Somewhere in the alley with the onions."

"Meat doesn't roll away."

"No, but it does get squished to oblivion when a sandal steps on it by accident."

Li Mei turned as red as a tomato. "Chinese men whip disobedient women on their butts until they beg for mercy. You are lucky I am a woman!"

Li Mei examined Kisa's cap. "Hmmm, very important. This cap is a sign of nobility." She bit the charm. "A pure gold He Xian-Gu, one of the Eight Immortals."

Georgi and Giselle leaned in close to look at the ornament. "Where did you find this ugly babe?" Li Mei said.

"She is *not* ugly!" Anya retorted. "Oh, yeah, I know. If we pretend she's not pretty, the ghosts will skip this house."

Li Mei uncurled Kisa's fists. She traced the lines from side to side. "She will cause the death of her father. I would like to wring his neck for forcing his wife to throw her away."

"I'm telling Mama the minute she walks in that Anya brought home a throwaway," Georgi taunted.

"No, you won't," Anya said. "You better not. If Mama knows, then Babushka knows. And then Dedushka will have another heart attack."

"Babushka will clobber all four of us," Giselle said.

"I am going to tell Papa. He will agree that it's our duty to save her," Anya said. "God only steals a girl's groceries when it's a matter of life and death."

"*Ai-yah.*" Li Mei shook her fist at Anya. "My groceries better be in your basket."

Anya looked at the floor tiles and didn't answer.

"Go upstairs and put Pidge in her cage. Fetch the talcum powder from your Babushka's dressing table. Tell her you need to blot your oily nose. Then come straight back down."

When Anya returned to the kitchen, Li Mei said, "Fill a pot with tap water and light the stove. We're making rice water so she won't dehydrate."

"Where do you keep the matches? And the pots?" Anya spun from one cupboard to the next.

"*Oy vey,*" Li Mei said. She unhooked a small copper pot from an S hook above the chopping block.

"Can't we give her more milk from the icebox?" Anya said.

"I told you, no cow's milk," Giselle said. "I'm late for my bath. I'll meet you tomorrow at nine to walk our birds. *If* I manage to sneak out."

"You didn't give her cow's milk, did you?" Li Mei frowned. "She's too young to digest it."

"She was starving."

Li Mei nudged Anya toward the pantry. "Bring me the bolt of cloth leaning against the wall. Lucky for you Buddha reminded me to oil the joints of the scissors this morning. Cut a couple squares about four times this size," she said, pointing to Kisa's bottom.

"I have a stack of diapers in my room."

"They're my cousin Davey's," Giselle said. "He won't miss them." She left through the kitchen door, blowing kisses to Anya as she crossed the courtyard.

"Good. Go get them. I won't have to waste the satin." Li Mei cradled Kisa in the crook of her arm. With her free hand, she filled the pot with water. "Measure a cup of pearl rice and toss in three pinches of sugar." She rubbed a wooden match against the striker to light the gas stove. "Your mother loves you, little one," Li Mei said, and kissed Kisa's forehead. "Instead of drowning you in the river, she brought you to Ani-ah."

Anya waited for the water to bubble. She chewed on a hangnail on her left thumb. So what if singers were supposed to keep their fingernails groomed. Who cared if Maestro Brodsky banged his baton on her wrist and banned her from the upcoming autumn recital. She refused to sit on the piano bench onstage with a spotlight burning her eyeballs. She tore the rest of the hangnail off with her teeth and sucked on her thumb to stop the bleeding.

Li Mei placed Kisa in a basket. "Miss Ani-ah, if you've got the urge to chew, try cud."

She scooped leftover kasha into a mixing bowl, then mashed the buckwheat groats with chopped egg. Georgi plugged his nose when he saw the egg yolks.

"Tell your rude brother to take his dislikes elsewhere. Lay Kisa down on the tea cloth, dust her bottom, and I'll show you how to put on a diaper. Don't get powder on her face or her wandering spirit won't recognize her when she wakes up."

Li Mei was an expert. She caught the ends of the square cloth together and fastened Kisa's nappy tight.

"Let me try now." Anya unclasped the pins and removed the diaper. She followed Li Mei's step-by-step instructions. Not bad for a first attempt.

"Now what, Li Mei?"

"Ride to Rue de Marco Polo for a pail of goat's milk. Rice water won't hold her." Li Mei pulled a ten-cent paper note from her waistband purse.

"After we feed her, I hope you know I am absolutely not putting her in the orphanage, even if Mama yells and threatens to—"

Li Mei wiped the tears from the corner of Anya's eyes with her dishrag. "Dandan and I will keep her in our room for the night. Tomorrow after I serve lunch, I'll take her on the trolley to Siccawei, and hand her over to my mother, Jia Li. The Jesuits will shelter her at the orphanage. While they pray to Jesus Christ, I will pray to the Jade Emperor to find this ugly girl a home."

"*Specibo*. Thank you." Anya corralled Li Mei and hugged her around her waist.

"Get another pomelo. I will cure your Mama with my secret extract so she'll stop fussing at her family."

"I ruined dinner. Mama will be furious."

"We will explain how this is my fault," Li Mei said. "We'll tell her I refused the meat because it was not up to her standards."

"But Mr. Katznelson always chooses the best for Mama. If the meat isn't full of flavor, he knows Mama will tell her friends and her friends will tell their friends and pretty soon everyone in Frenchtown *and* the International Settlement will know. Mama will suspect you are lying."

"No lie. The meat is covered with flies by now, if a beggar hasn't already devoured it raw. Now scram. I have work to do. *Catchee chop-chop*."

Anya pretended she was Li Mei's servant and bowed. "Papa doesn't allow pidgin English in this house. I'm telling him you broke the rule."

"Tell him if you dare. *Chop-chop*, Miss Ani-ah."

"Mama doesn't want me to overexert in this weather." Anya headed to the closet for her camera.

"Be at this kitchen door before half past six or you'll catch it from me *and* your Mama," Li Mei yelled, whacking her rolling pin on the wood block.

Li Mei knows how important this day is, Anya thought. *She is my friend.*

seven

Anya stepped through the creaky gate backward the way Babushka taught her to when she was a toddler. Mama said Babushka was ridiculously superstitious, gossiping with friends on a park bench, tying and retying the kerchiefs that covered their hair, predicting bad omens and the end of the world, carrying a parasol, rain or shine. But Dedushka remembered the old days, before Jew haters pelted Jewish store windows with rocks, yelling "Filthy Yid, leave us alone and return to Jerusalem." He remembered when Babushka still danced around the six-foot-tall sunflowers in her garden. It was a time before Dedushka lost his thumbs for refusing to join the czar's army and still held hands with his beautiful bride.

Chen tipped his black cap at Anya. *How do his white gloves and tuxedo remain spotless?* He resumed waxing the big black Buick as he did every Friday before sundown.

At the corner, Anya crossed into a crush of Chinese refugees beating gongs and ringing bells, their heads twitching like gnats, necks thrust forward as if a cowboy had lassoed them and was pulling them to move faster. It sounded to Anya like all ten radio stations in the city were blasting at once, like the whole world was bombarding downtown Shanghai.

A warning whistle from a French *gendarme* alarmed her to stop, which saved her from crashing into a coolie pulling a boy in a fancy sedan chair. She had momentarily forgotten Shanghai's drive-to-the-left rule.

"Anya, is that you?" A voice she recognized called out from behind the fringes. "Stop, Xi!"

The coolie halted and carefully laid down the handles of the chair. Unlike most drivers, he wore a tailored uniform. He helped his master from the padded seat.

Bobby Sassoon! Anya felt dizzy. *Wait until I tell Giselle! She will plotz onto the ground.*

Bobby strode to Anya's side. This was the first time Anya had been alone with Bobby, although one could hardly call this alone. His sparkly eyes reminded her of Papa's when he came home from work and saw Mama after a long day.

Bobby Sassoon has a crush on me?

"Why haven't you been at bowling club lately? No one else on the team scores as many strikes as you," Bobby said.

"My mother is terrified that any place with six lanes and eight-pound black balls might crush my piano fingers!"

Bobby's dimples were much more obvious when he smiled. Yes, he just might be her soul mate, the boy she was destined to date.

"Is that why you're not coming to my party?"

"Your party?"

"My birthday party on Tuesday! My bowling party. You didn't receive my invitation?" Bobby said.

"You don't know my address."

"Where the prettiest and sweetest girl in Frenchtown lives is definitely my business." He smiled at Anya, then scrunched his forehead. "Xi! Did you deliver all twelve of the invitations I sent with you?"

"Yes, Master Bobby." Xi's eyes darted around.

When Georgi was lying, his eyes looked everywhere but at Mama, especially if he was hiding something big.

"You delivered to Rue de Victor Emmanuel, to Anya Rosen's house? Right?" Bobby asked.

Xi stood still and didn't answer. The right side of his upper lip pulled straight and twitched, slightly baring his teeth. Another giveaway that he wasn't telling the truth.

Bobby put his hands on his hips. "Answer me."

"I cannot, Master Bobby." Xi dropped his head.

Bobby's face grew red. "You lost the invitation."

Xi trembled at Bobby's angry accusation. "Madame Sassoon fished through the pile. She took one. She threw it in the garbage."

Bobby shook his head. "This is *my* birthday. My party. I invite whomever I want, including Russians—" He stopped midsentence. "I'm sorry, Anya. My father caught a Russian sneaking into the Canidrome for the dog races. The man cheated on his bets. Now Father says all Ashkenazim are thieves."

"We are not thieves!" Anya retorted. But it wasn't Bobby's fault his father was a bigot. "It's the same in my family, only it's my grandmother who has decided not to like the Sephardim."

Once when Anya asked Babushka why she never said hello to the Sephardic grandmothers in the shops, she blurted, "Oriental Jews are not white and they made their fortunes trading opium. They are a bad influence. Amen." Babushka had spoken with a grudge in her voice, as though her people and Bobby's people had quarreled, like the families of Romeo Montague and Juliet Capulet.

Anya changed the subject quickly. "What's so great about dogs racing?"

"Want to come and see sometime?"

"My father will never let me. He thinks all Sephardic gamblers are *schlimazels*."

"Touché! You've got spunk, Anya."

"By the way, I consider myself Odessan, not Russian."

"What's the difference?"

"If you'd lived on the Black Sea in Odessa, you'd know."

"You are Ashkenazi?"

"Yes."

"Then there is no difference as far as my parents are concerned." Bobby frowned as he said, "I guess we have two strikes against us."

Did I hear that correctly? Bobby called us us. A silly half giggle lurched by the lump in Anya's throat. *I am going to that party, with or without a fancy printed invitation.*

"Speaking of strikes, what time is your party?"

"A girl with a witty mind." Bobby winked at her. "I like that."

Anya couldn't breathe. She felt giddy.

"Two p.m. Tuesday. Don't bring a gift. Just bring you." Bobby jumped in the sedan chair. "Home, now," he ordered Xi.

Anya waited until Bobby's chair rolled out of sight to hoot and jump in the air. *He likes me. Will he ask me to the movies after his party?* Bobby and Anya strolling arm and arm through French Park. Sitting down on a bench. Bobby kissing her cheek softly and asking her to be his girlfriend by pinning a pearl brooch on her blouse. She would wear the pin to school to show the world she was Bobby Sassoon's girl. Mama would say, "Anya Rosen, that pin better not leave holes in your cashmere sweater. Do you know how many newspaper articles your Papa has to publish in order for us to afford that one twinset for you?"

What was the point? Bobby was a Sephardic Jew. He couldn't pass as a regular Jew. His hair was jet black and his skin and eyes were dark brown. If she invited him for Shabbat dinner, he'd pronounce the Hebrew incorrectly, wouldn't use a fork, and would chant different prayers. *"What's in a name? That which we call a rose / By any other name would smell as sweet." Juliet said that about Romeo.* Two thousand years ago, Bobby's ancestors were Pharaoh's slaves in Egypt, like hers were. So what if his family settled in Baghdad and hers sailed the extra miles across the Black Sea to Odessa? *A Jew is a Jew.*

I will attend that party. Period. By Tuesday she would think up clever remarks and a few jokes with punch lines she'd remember, for once. She bet he'd split his sides if she asked him, "Why do you Sephardic people eat rice with your hands at Passover?"

Rice. Rice water. Goat milk! I better get moving.

When Anya arrived at the Marco Polo Market, she avoided Sara Tukachinsky's father, the policeman whose post was the west gate. She rode through the east entrance. She didn't want to answer questions from a man standing on a pile of sandbags, wearing shorts, with hairier legs than Dedushka's.

Up and down the dusty aisles, Anya searched for pomelos and goat milk. She rushed past fishy-smelling tubs and rows of willow pattern porcelain arranged neatly on blankets. She didn't buy a bag of roasted peanuts in the shell, although her mouth watered. A few scrawny chickens pecked at watermelon seeds littering the pavement. They clucked as they snacked at the base of baskets holding eggs gathered this morning from village coops.

She bought two pomelos for the price of one. Not a single goat was tied to the posts. In her most polite voice, she asked each seller, "Do you have any goat milk left, by chance, for my baby?" When the last vendor shook his head, she stomped like Georgi would. The merchant looked at her with blank eyes and continued wiping his empty pails with a brown burlap rag.

A gruff voice, with an American accent, spoke from behind her, "You are much too young to be a mother."

Anya whirled around. The Caucasian man, dressed in a beige tunic and baggy matching trousers, was wearing penny loafers without socks, and no penny. His head was shaved except for a black ponytail, streaked with gray, hanging down to his waist.

"There is a dehydrated baby girl in my mama's kitchen."

"She is your sister?"

"Not my blood sister."

"To whom does she belong?"

"I. Don't. Know." This rude man was wasting her precious time.

"Wait." He extended his hand to shake. "Dr. Joseph Miller.

I built the Battle Creek Sanitarium. With funding from Madame C."

"Madame Chiang Kai-shek?"

He nodded with reverence in his eyes, as if the Madame was a goddess. "With her patronage, I invented a machine that extracts liquid from soybeans. This will feed many starving children. I predict that the Chinese will soon call soy 'the cow of China.'"

"Are soys as good as goats?" Anya asked.

Dr. Miller chuckled. "No, funny mother. Soy is a bean, not an animal."

"How do I know it's not poison? Has it been sterilized? My mama doesn't allow me to eat from the street." Mama had warned her never to speak with strangers but she didn't care what Mama said. This stranger was a doctor.

"You'll have to trust me."

He offered her a cup filled with a creamy liquid. She sipped, then gulped. She was so thirsty and the milk was sweet and tasted like plain old cow's milk. But better.

"I like this soy," Anya said, smiling at the man. "I hope your invention is a success. Will you bring it to the United States? When I'm seventeen, I'm traveling to New York."

"Someday I'll return to America. For now, I'm needed in Shanghai."

"I have lots of ideas, too. Big ones. I want to lead an important life like my aunt Paulina's. She's the first doctor in our family."

"A woman doctor. In China?"

"No, she lives in San Francisco. That's in California, on the west coast of America where rolling hills are golden and orange trees grow on every corner and—"

"What is your name, girl-to-be-reckoned-with?"

"Anya Rosengart—I-I mean, Rosen. But when I get to America, I am changing my name again. To Anna Rose. Not Anna. AH-na."

"Tell me, AH-na Rose, what will happen to your little one when you leave Shanghai?"

"Kisa will have a real family before I leave. I found her in a basket in the gutter. An awful mother threw her away."

Dr. Miller didn't seem shocked by this news. His reassuring expression reminded her of Papa. "Please bring this child, who just might grow up because of your courage, to my clinic for a checkup tomorrow. I'd like to check her bilirubin and make sure she's hasn't contracted any diseases."

"On the Sabbath, it is forbidden to exchange money. But thank you anyway."

"The exam will be free. My clinic is near Great World on Rue du Weikwei." He curled her fingers around the wire handle of a pail. "In the meantime, turn your Kisa into a fan of my soy milk."

The wind suddenly gusted, pushing against Anya like an impatient amah chasing disobedient children through the park. She shivered from the slight chill in the air. *Finally, I will sleep in a cool bed.* She walked slowly so she wouldn't spill a drop.

"*Specibo*—I mean, thank you, Dr. Miller," she called over her shoulder.

"You are welcome, AH-na. *Do svidanya.* See you tomorrow."

eight

When Anya walked up the driveway, Pearl had already whisked the flowerpots, lawn furniture, and croquet set into storage. Chen had taped the windowpanes and inserted reinforced shutters. She climbed the steps to the front door and scurried to the kitchen. She found Li Mei feeding Kisa rice water with a dropper.

"You were gone over half an hour, slowpoke," Li Mei said.

Anya set the pail and pair of pomelos in the sink. "Bobby Sassoon kidnapped me."

"Don't lie to me."

"He invited me to his birthday party."

"I hope it's not a swimming party."

"Bowling."

"Good. It's too dangerous to swim during the month of the Hungry Ghost Moon. A ghost is waiting at the bottom of every pool to drown children."

"If I believed everything you told me, I'd hide under the covers all month. Anyway, there were no goats. But I met a doctor from America who gave us soy milk for Kisa."

"How dare you waste your papa's hard-earned money!" Li Mei scowled.

Anya dipped a teaspoon in the pail. "Try a sip. Dr. Miller didn't ask me for one coin. And he's checking Kisa's billy rubies tomorrow at his free clinic."

Li Mei rolled her eyes, and said, "For now, Ugly will drink your friend's fake milk. When she gets to Siccawei, my mother will switch her to goat milk." She blew softly on Kisa's cheek. "What are billy rubies? Sounds like jewels for a goat."

"No idea. We'll find out tomorrow."

Li Mei placed Kisa on a bed of tea towels. She shook the pomelos, then cut both in half. She was straining the liquid from the fruit into sesame bath oil when Papa's loud footsteps headed toward the kitchen. Anya and Li Mei exchanged a panicked look as they waited—prayed—for him to climb the stairs, two by two, to his bedroom to dress for Shabbat. Li Mei dropped the strainer and scooped Kisa into her arms, and the jolt produced a cry that quickly turned into wailing.

"Mystery solved." Papa burst through the kitchen door followed by Georgi. "I assumed the squall was a parade of babies rolling by outside in prams."

Anya sucked in a breath and braced for Kisa's doom. *This is it. Why couldn't Georgi divert Papa's attention instead of standing there with bug eyes?*

"Whose little darling is this?" Papa asked. He put on his spectacles and placed one of Kisa's tiny hands on his palm.

"Ask your daughter, Master Josh," Li Mei said. She put the tip of the dropper in the bowl of milk and squeezed the black bulb to fill it.

Papa's left eyebrow raised and his nostril twitched like a rabbit's nose. He looked at Anya, waiting for her answer.

"Her mother is missing. I found her in the gutter and I named her Kisa because she mews like a pussycat." Anya darted a look at Li Mei for reassurance. Li Mei patted the good luck phoenix embroidered on her sleeve and dribbled some milk into Kisa's rosebud mouth.

Papa stopped tapping his loafer on the tile floor. "Who do you think you are, Anya? Pharaoh's wife?" Papa's eyes pierced hers.

Why does Papa bring the Bible into every problem?

"This is not Moses!" Papa shouted.

The creak of the door made Anya jump. A hint of Chanel No. 5 perfume preceded Mama.

"Moses is here? In time for Shabbat?" Mama chuckled. She walked into the room, struggling with the zipper of an emerald green drop-waist dress. The door swung to meet the frame, squeaking at its hinges, and fluttered, then closed and was still.

Oh God, Anya screamed silently. *I'm finished now. When I walk in the valley of the shadow of death. . . .* She closed her eyes and braced for the uproar.

"What a beautiful newborn," Mama said. "*Mes deux bébés* were once this delicate."

Papa whistled at Mama.

"Zip me up, for God's sake," Mama said.

He released the teeth of the zipper stuck at her waist and pulled it up without catching any of Mama's stray blond hairs.

"Your dress matches your bright eyes." Papa kissed the top of Mama's French bun. She shrugged like there was a cramp in her shoulder muscle.

"We don't pay you to babysit other people's children, Li Mei," she said.

"It's Anya's baby," Georgi said, pointing at his sister like she was a two-headed Cyclops. "She dragged the baby in from the alley and she's keeping her."

Anya clutched her head. Mama's heels clicked, sounding like machine guns firing rounds across the river. "Oh my God, Rosengartner. Are you involved in this debauchery!"

Anya bristled as her mother addressed her father.

Why can't Mama throw away the silly old Russian customs about what name a wife may call her husband in front of servants? We live in China now.

"Anya, have you lost your mind? What if the mother had cholera and gave birth to her in a doorway?" Mama cried.

"There's a foundling home nearby," Papa offered.

"I went to that foundling home first. They let girl babies die," Anya said.

Li Mei nodded her head.

Mama unhooked a whisk from the utensil holder next to the *piroshki* assembly and squeezed it until her knuckles paled. Anya pressed up against the wood block. Mama wouldn't hit her, but her fury alarmed Anya.

Georgi barreled into Mama. "Don't be mad at Anya. She's a

good girl," he pleaded, patting her back. Mama recoiled and nudged him from her waist.

Papa paced from the pantry to the sink to the stove to the pantry. Li Mei's jaws were clenched, and twitching.

"This poor child's parents placed little value on her life. Anya could not witness this atrocity and do nothing. That is good," Papa said. "Give me a moment to think."

Mama picked up one of the dough patties. Chunks of buckwheat and chopped egg sprinkled the floor. "Kasha? I ordered sirloin beef," she said, shaking her head. "We do not serve buckwheat on Shabbat."

"Mr. Katznelson's meat was too bloody to serve in your kosher house," Li Mei said.

She is lying to Mama to save me from two punishments.

"But I taught you how to remove blood from meat using salt. Did you run out?"

"No, Madame, the salt barrel is full."

"I've never had a problem with Mr. Katznelson's meat before."

"He must have added blood to make the beef look fresher."

Mama rolled her eyes. "Because you leave me no choice, we will eat this *dreck* tonight."

"Stella! Stop swearing," Papa said. His chest protruded like a sergeant. "Li Mei is a human being and she takes good care of us."

"Of course she does, but right now she deserves a reprimand," Mama said.

Li Mei pushed her shoulders forward and rose onto her tiptoes. "Tonight in Tianjin," Li Mei half whispered, "the women will pluck off the wings and hind legs of four-inch-long locusts, then fry them alive in rancid oil. No wheat, millet, and rice remain in the fields because the locusts devoured every last grain. Do you know what that hunger feels like in the pit of your stomach?"

Anya and Georgi shrank back and Papa grimaced. This was good-bye to Li Mei. Surely Mama would fire her.

But Mama ignored the cook. With her hands on her hips, she said, "Rosengartner, if that baby dies in our kitchen, a Chinese spirit might snatch *our* baby to keep her company."

"Stella, when did you become so superstitious? No one will kidnap Georgi. I promise." Papa folded his arms across his chest. "Our daughter is right. This baby girl is our responsibility. Saving her is like saving the whole world. That's what the Talmud says about this perplexing situation."

Papa took Mama's hand and stroked it. "Blessed are You, Hashem, our God, King of the Universe, who created this woman more beautiful than any other in *my* universe." Papa held his hands together at his chest and dipped his knees, rocking in awe of Mama.

"You are like a fool who lifts a rock, then drops it on his own foot," Mama yelled.

"Shame on you," Papa said, his eyes wet with hurt.

"Li Mei, I don't care how you do it, but I beg you, remove the girl from these premises," Mama whimpered, clutching her abdomen. "I am pregnant."

Li Mei squealed. Anya, Papa, and Georgi searched Mama's face, then one another's. Anya didn't know whether to hug Mama or run from the room.

"Oh, Madame Stella, I knew it! *Now* we understand why you've behaved like a whirling dervish."

Their excitement reminded Anya of the last moments before the family finished their jigsaw puzzle. Georgi and Dedushka would hold what they each called "the last piece" but neither of them were willing to lay his down first on the game table.

"Let me show you how I knew Madame was expecting."

Li Mei gripped Papa's wrist and led the whole family outside to a patch of loam below the windowsill. She pointed to three tiny bamboo shoots knuckling through the earth. Li Mei bowed to the ground and then at Mama. "New bamboo growing in the garden means new baby growing in the missus. Soon your belly will swell round as a watermelon."

The folds of Mama's billowy dresses had hidden her stomach. That is why no one had noticed. Any day now, the buttons of her housecoat would pop out of the buttonholes, like they had when she was pregnant with Georgi, and skitter across the oak floor.

"Mama, I will share my room if it's a girl, and my sister sleeps in her own crib, and doesn't wet my bed." Anya laid her head on Mama's shoulder.

"Your papa said life would be easier in China. But it isn't. Everything I do is much more difficult here," Mama said. "And this city is ugly and noisy and crowded and I'm so very tired." Mama slumped on the garden stool. "I don't blame you, Anya, for feeling terrible for this abandoned baby, but your decision to bring her home was misguided. Joshua, please transport her from our house."

Anya reached out to unfurl Mama's clenched fingers and hold her hand. But Mama pulled away, stood up, and disappeared through the kitchen door.

I will not allow Papa to throw out Kisa—not ever.

"When we return from *shul*, we'll say our blessings, eat dinner, and play cards with our guests. Li Mei, I expect you to . . . *handle* this situation." Papa's stern tone quickly melted. "Congratulations, Anya and Georgi. You will soon have a baby brother or sister to play with!" Papa threw his arms into the air and clapped at the skies. "Now young man, let's go!" He led Georgi from the courtyard. "Get your Dedushka. We don't want to miss Rabbi Mendel's *maariv* prayer."

Li Mei and Anya walked back into the kitchen. "I will babysit until the *piroshki* is in the oven," Anya said, and lifted Kisa from her basket.

"If I wasn't on the verge of losing my job, I would decline your helpful invitation."

Li Mei lit the burner, covered the flame with her frying pan, and poured in the oil. The *piroshki* browned, and Anya could almost taste the crunchy dough.

"*Ai-yah!* Move Kisa away! The oil is sputtering."

"Li Mei. You are *my* servant," Anya said with a smile, "not the other way around."

"Plucky girl. I guess the cat spit out your tongue."

Before Anya could reply, Li Mei said in a mock-stern tone, "I am in charge of this kitchen. Get out now. Take Kisa upstairs. I need to concentrate."

nine

*A*nya made a beeline to her bedroom, slammed the door, and locked it. She emptied her bottom dresser drawer, the deepest of the five, and lined it with her silk robe. After she placed Kisa inside the folds and directed her to settle down and go to sleep, she reached into her closet, her safe place. She pulled from a fat wooden hanger one of Babushka's furs, stored in there because Babushka's closet was too small for her fox and mink stoles. Anya slinked to the tall pedestal mirror like a magnificent silver fox. Clamping her mammoth jaws over Kisa's father's imaginary head, she growled, "No mother is more ferocious than I."

She stooped to pick Kisa up and nuzzled her into the soft fur. "When I journey to America, I will bring you with me. We'll be known as Kisa and Anna Rose, and I'll never call you a throwaway or admit that I'm a Jew." Anya stroked Kisa's cheek softly, with one finger. "Mama made me leave behind my *matryoshka* collection in Odessa with Luba. When I get the dolls back, I will give half of them to you and we will line them up on the window ledge of your room. Wherever you live."

Kisa burped in her sleep but slumbered peacefully.

"Can I tell you a secret?" Anya placed her palm over Kisa's heart and felt the warm skin rise and fall, rise and fall. "I left my Russian soul with my dolls. The largest one I own is decorated with dog-rose flowers. The twenty-fifth doll is miniscule and doesn't open. It's as tiny as my pinkie fingernail. So I put my soul inside the twenty-fourth smallest doll."

She sat down on the bench of her mahogany vanity, adjusted the two side mirrors, and then peered at her profile and the back of her head. It wasn't fair that Georgi got to bring his warrior doll, Bogatyr, to Shanghai. *Georgi gets whatever he wants.*

Luba wouldn't recognize Anya's face reflected from the oval mirror: her hair was as unruly as Medusa's, her cheeks were splotched. She felt tingles run up and down her thighs and the small of her back, thinking of her surprise meeting with Bobby on Avenue Fouchon.

The scrape on her cheek from her tumble was barely visible. She dabbed it with powder and patted down her frizzy hair. No matter how much pomade she applied, her hair misbehaved. The acne on her nose had disappeared after three applications of Li Mei's herbal paste. Babushka would have no reason now to label her a low-class girl and apply mounds of concealer to her outbreak. *How did Mama grow up in her house and not think she was an ugly duckling?*

Mirror, mirror on the wall,
Who's the fairest of them all?

Since *Snow White and the Seven Dwarves* won the Academy Award, she and Giselle had repeated the queen's monologue, then pointed at each other and mocked, "Not you." But Giselle *was* the prettiest girl in Frenchtown, with straight blond hair, almond-shaped brown eyes, and smooth and creamy skin without blemishes.

There was a loud knock on Anya's door. The doorknob jiggled. Another knock. A pound.

"Go away, Georgi."

"Anya Rosengartner. Unlock this door."

No. No. No, she mouthed at the door standing between her and Babushka. *Mama must have spilled the beans.*

"You are not allowed to lock your door. What if you fainted and hit your head? Amen."

Anya sucked in her breath.

"Anushkina, please. Answer me."

"Papa gave me a new name, Anya Rosen, and he makes the rules in this house."

Three more whacks, and then a terrible sound like a broken bottle crashing to the floor. Crystal shards from the doorknob skittered under the door. Anya dug her fingernails into the skin on her palms.

Babushka pushed her hand through the hole where the knob had been, turned the lock, and slapped the door against the wall, denting the floral wallpaper. She was holding a hammer.

"Look what you made me do, Anya," she yelled, her cheeks flaming as red as her kerchief.

"Babushka. Put that hammer down."

"Why are you wearing my fox?" She dropped the tool on the rug and pulled at the coat sleeve.

Anya clung to the fur like a leech. Kisa started to wail.

"If you don't take that infant out of this house, your mama has Papa's permission to return your bike."

"She wouldn't."

"She begged me to reason with you. She doesn't have the energy to argue tonight."

"Did Georgi leave for *shul* with Papa?"

"Of course he went. He has plenty to memorize for his bar mitzvah."

"His ceremony isn't for three years. Why didn't I have a *brit milah* when I turned thirteen? Why do boys get all the privileges?"

Anya struggled out of the sleeves and Babushka draped the limp coat over her shoulder and shuffled to her bedroom. Hangers clapped across the pole in her closet. She sneezed three times in a row.

Anya picked Kisa up and rocked her until she calmed. She put her down in the bureau bed, then turned in circles in the middle of her rug, one foot in front of the other as she followed the inside edge of the weave's black swirl pattern. *I will think for myself. It is not forbidden to think.* Sweat dripped from her forehead. Babushka and Mama together were like a monsoon. They would persuade Papa to call the coolies tonight after dinner. When Babushka loomed closer, Anya's thoughts and words muddled. She had this unsettling effect on Dedushka, too. She made the coarse gray hairs in his eyebrows twitch. He seemed to shrink like a wrinkled fig.

Anya kneeled to remake her bed, folding and tucking in each corner and glided her hand over the sheets and coverlet to remove the creases. If she did a perfect job, Babushka might not notice Kisa's poop stain.

A door slammed. Babushka's footsteps headed to Anya's room. She stood at the door with her hands on her hips.

Anya scampered across the rug and stepped on a jagged piece of glass. She didn't feel pain until the cut oozed.

"I'm sorry I picked up the baby, Babushka. And I'm not sorry, too. Li Mei will bring Kisa to Jia Li at Siccawei tomorrow. Please don't let Mama or Papa call the coolies to take her away."

Babushka stood straight as a flagpole and pointed at the swath of blood staining the Persian rug. The cut stung and throbbed. Anya hung her head. She kneeled down on the carpet and brushed Babushka's ankles with her fingertips. "Please don't let them kill Kisa."

Could she prove she was mature, not a stupid crybaby? Sobs reverberated in her throat. *I did not cry in Odessa.* She couldn't stop herself.

"Save your dramatics for the opera house," Babushka said.

"I won't."

Let Babushka decipher what that meant. Should she tell her grandmother about her dreams, the ones that grew inside her own mind? *I could tell her that I want to travel around the world, not get married at twenty, be a photojournalist, or a doctor, or an inventor. Anything but sing opera.*

She organized her thoughts and drummed up her courage, but then Mama appeared at the door.

"Take Kisa down to the servant's rooms and clean up the mess you made. Mamochka, come out of there." Her voice was calm. She stepped aside so Babushka could leave the room. "Take your *Shabbos* bath, Anya," she said, and shut the door.

A door closed in Anya's face by Mama meant she wouldn't talk to her for a few hours. Then, as if the afternoon hadn't been ruined by her temper, she'd speak in a polite tone, until the next time Anya infuriated her.

Anya retrieved a starched linen handkerchief from the pile on her dresser. She wiped her heel. Bloody polka dots seeped like ink through the stiff cloth. *The stains will never wash out and I don't care.* Babushka would admonish her. "May you repent for ruining this fine linen. Amen." But Anya pressed the cloth harder against her wound. What did a small white square matter in the face of Chinese fathers throwing away babies? She held it over her heel for a few minutes until, with a final squeeze, the bleeding stopped.

Anya waited in the hall for steam to escape from underneath Mama's door. Then she limped to the kitchen with Kisa asleep in her arms.

"Food is on the way," she whispered. "More milk and you'll be a happy girl."

Georgi tripped over his shoelace running toward her. "Show me how to hold her."

"Uh-uh. She might poop on your dress shirt. Why aren't you in *shul*, Mr. Klutz?" Anya said, shaking her head.

"If you trot, you can catch up with your papa, Joji," Li Mei said. "He just turned the corner."

"Give me Kisa." Li Mei handed Anya a pear-shaped vial and a sprig of leaves and curled her fingers around it. "Put a thimbleful into your mama's bath water. Slosh it around so it mixes well. Tell Madame Stella the oil is an ancient Chinese balm for jade-smooth skin. Put the pomelo leaves under her mattress." Li Mei's voice softened. "One day we will tell her the magic pomelo stopped her hollering and gave life to her happiness spirit."

Anya was halfway up the stairway when she remembered Jules's message. She trotted down the steps. "I owe you a big favor because you didn't tell Mama the truth about the meat."

Li Mei bowed. "I gave you my word."

She curtsied like a princess as Anya had taught her. "Don't say another word about Kisa. Go now. Cure your mama."

"By the way, Jules sent his regards, and I quote: 'To beautiful Li Mei.'"

Li Mei flushed from her neck up to her cheeks, the color of the Shabbat wine. She whipped around and fished the last batch of perfectly browned *piroshki* from the crackling oil.

Anya slipped into Mama's bathroom and hid behind the towel rack. She would wait until Mama stripped off her slip and unclasped her bra and sunk into the water before she added the oil. Mama's reflection in the floor-to-ceiling mirror showed smooth arms, the color of ivory, like the Hollywood starlet Deanna Durbin's. Slender legs, curvaceous hips, and a skinny waist that wasn't as narrow as the last time Anya spied on Mama. There was a faint outline of a bulge in her belly like the eastern curve of the waxing moon. Mama inserted four ivory hairpins into her French bun and tucked in a couple of stray hairs. She turned to the side and placed her hands over her belly, tracing the skin as though she was searching for a clue. She was smiling.

One of Anya's shoes squeaked on the marble floor. Mama covered her breasts with her arm and grasped a white bath towel with her other hand. Anya stood up, embarrassed she had been exposed.

"You must knock first, Anush. I expect privacy when I'm bathing. You know better."

"I brought you a special potion from Li Mei for silky skin. Smell," Anya said, and waved the glass bottle under Mama's nose.

Mama took a whiff and closed her eyes. When she liked an aroma, her face softened into a kind of rapture, as though the smell had wrapped her in the warm, plush towel. Anya's trespass was forgiven. Mama dipped her toe into the steaming bath water. Her forehead loosened and her head tumbled forward. "What is it, that familiar smell? You and Li Mei are trying to make up to me, aren't you?"

"Get in, Mama. It's pomelo oil. You have loads of time to relax before we light the candles. Let me rub your shoulders."

"No, thank you, Anush. I'm not in the mood for anyone to touch me."

"Tell me again about the opera house in Milan," Anya said, as Mama stepped into the hot water. Even though Anya had been avoiding talk of singing, number one on the list of Mama pleasers was showing great interest in her descriptions of the most recent city she had toured with the opera. Mama's eyes sparkled when she remembered clean, polished floors in museums, gondolas on waterways, La Scala's velvet seats, and the sculpture of four panthers drawing Melpomene, the muse of tragedy, in a chariot.

"Not now, Anush. Let me be."

Mama hadn't cracked the window before she turned on the hot water, and each humid breath Anya inhaled tasted like citrus rind and Mama's sweat. Anya fingered the waxy leaves in her pocket. *Mama doesn't know me anymore.* She shut the bathroom door, and as she walked across the soft rug to her parents' bed, wondered why the woman in the bathtub had become almost a stranger. She struggled to lift the mattress and dropped it twice before she was able to stuff the leaves under a corner and flop the mattress in place. Out puffed a cloud of dust that tickled her nose, and she sneezed. *Dandan forgot to shake the feather beds again. If she keeps shirking her duties, Mama and Babushka will replace her with a younger* amah. Why did dust motes in China irritate Mama's eyes so much when in Odessa she never had allergies?

ten

*A*nya had asked Papa the same question she asked every Friday. Why can't I go to *shul*, too? Dedushka always blurted that *shul* was no place for a girl. Anya must stay at home and prepare for Shabbat. He'd hold his deformed hands in front of her face as if the sight of the missing thumbs would scare her off. *Old-fashioned, that's what grandfathers are. The old folks should have been left behind in Odessa.* She imagined a city of *kvetching* old ladies and their husbands, and giggled, but covered her mouth before Babushka pried into her thoughts and made her feel guilty.

At the synagogue on Seymour Road, Papa, Dedushka, and Georgi—and the rest of the Jewish men who had escaped to Shanghai with their families—were welcoming the Shabbat Bride, without her. Wrapped in their *tallit*, they would turn to the east toward Jerusalem and sing, "*L'cha dodi.* Come, O bride, come," and watch her float down from Heaven to reign over the world for one day. There were only two synagogues to choose from in Shanghai, one for the Ashkenazim, one for the Sephardim. At home in Odessa, seventy synagogues divided by profession lined Malaya Arnautskaya, the street for synagogues. Luba's father, a banker, worshipped on the south side, while Lily's father, a baker, went to services a couple of blocks away on the southwestern corner.

The hand of the clock clicked to 7:26. It was eighteen minutes before sunset, the commanded time for women to kindle the Sabbath lights.

"*Maydelas*, move closer to me," Babushka said, linking arms with Mama and Anya. In Odessa, they lit their candles in the pantry in secret, away from the prying eyes of anti-Semitic neighbors. The candle table in Shanghai stood proudly in front of the window at Papa's insistence: "May the eyes of the world witness our golden candlelight. It is a *mitzvah*, to celebrate Judaism openly."

Because of the storm alert, Mo-chou had moved the half-moon-shaped table covered with an embroidered cloth to the center of the living room. They circled the three pairs of beeswax candles in silver candleholders. Anya ducked to the other side of Mama to avoid the smell of Babushka's bad breath.

They slipped coins into the slot in the ceramic *pushka* decorated with doves. When the charity box was full, Papa planned to send the *tzedakah* to the Zionists to reestablish Israel where Jews would live in peace.

"Take off your kerchief, Mamochka," Mama said. "You're annoying me with your modesty."

Babushka stuck her fingers in her ears and grimaced, then tightened her paisley scarf. The edges of cloth had mopped up

84

the sweat that beaded around her forehead and was a darker hue. She pulled her tattered shawl over her hunched shoulders. Babushka preferred to wear her old clothes and refused Mama's gifts from Avenue du Jardin. Her veined hands shook as she nudged the wooden matchbox drawer open. She couldn't seem to pinch the matchstick between her gnarled fingers.

Mama helped Babushka light the wicks and then, waving her arms like a prima donna onstage, lit her own pair of candles. *She was born to make a spectacle.*

Anya lit hers last, one candle for *shamor*, observance, and one for *zachor*, remembrance. It was time for her second *neshamah* to enter her body. Her skin tingled with the feeling of the additional soul slipping in. This extra soul might distract her from her worries about the Japanese and Chinese fighting for control of Shanghai. And Chinese fathers leaving useless girls to die. And the Nazis forbidding Jewish children to attend school and swim in community pools. And what Anya's new school year would bring.

Mama waved her hands over the flames three times to welcome the light of Shabbat into her heart, then covered her eyes and recited an ancient blessing. The Talmud ordered women to light Shabbat candles to make up for Eve's sin of tempting the snake in the Garden of Eden. Her act had dimmed the world's light. *The Talmud has more rules and punishments than Babushka,* Anya thought.

As they stood together in the candlelight, raindrops pattered on the windowpanes, at first softly—the sound of relief—then a downpour. Filaments of smoke swirled to the ceiling and vaporized. Anya squinted her eyes at the six flaming wicks. In

Odessa, dusk had been her and Mama's favorite time during Shabbat. They would zip each other's lace party dresses. If the Shabbat fell on a family birthday, they wore taffeta gowns from the collection bought for Mama's opening-night opera parties. After Mama applied her own eyeliner, rouge, and lipstick, she would swish pink blush along the curve of Anya's cheekbones. Then they slipped into *peau-de-soir* pumps, and creaked open the hope chest to chose a selection of silk cushions for the sofas. Anya lined the fireplace mantel with clove- and vanilla-scented candles while Mama filled bowls with pears, peaches, tangerines, whatever fruit was in season. Valentina lit the fire, except in summer, when she placed four candles in the fireplace. Anya arranged candied violets on a sterling platter. In Odessa, Mama didn't sigh if the rows weren't straight. Before they lit the candles, Mama dropped one half of a chocolate truffle on Anya's tongue and popped the other half into her own mouth. In Odessa, Babushka celebrated Shabbos in her own apartment surrounded by her sisters, Manya and Lara, and their daughters.

The words "I smell Shabbat" wrenched Anya from her memories of Odessa. Papa's voice bellowed in a come-and-meet-our-guests baritone. Anya hurried to the foyer to greet him and helped him out of his dripping raincoat. Dedushka kissed the tips of his fingers, then tapped the mezuzah on the door frame. The scroll inside the aquamarine glass box—still placed too high for Georgi to reach—was inscribed with prayers to protect the family's comings and goings. Babushka had given Mama and Papa five mezuzahs on their wedding day, including two for the nurseries of a boy and girl, in that order. He waited until just before sunset on their first Shabbat in Shanghai to nail them to the doorposts and chant the *Shehekiyanu*—the prayer of gratitude to God for bringing them to this wonderful moment. He had faced Mama and bowed, slid one step to the right, pirouetted, and sprang onto his left foot. The whole family clapped as Papa danced the *mazurka*, flinging his arms above his head and singing, "Jews live here."

Anya hugged Dedushka first because he was the eldest. He stood as straight as an Imperial soldier, stiff arms glued to his sides. Witnessing his friends' deaths in the Great War had hardened Dedushka's heart.

I won't ever stop loving my relatives because of a war, Anya had resolved. *Isn't impending death a good reason to show affection when you're alive?*

Next Anya wrapped her arms around Papa's chest. For someone with such a big appetite, he weighed ten pounds less than Mama. And Mama was *not* fat. She always sucked in her belly to make it flat. But now there was a good reason for the little pooch around her belly button.

A tall man tossed his hat at the rack. It landed and twirled around the wooden arm. "*Grazioso*," he exclaimed.

Wash, wash, slosh, he stepped into the foyer, followed by a boy.

"You are dripping on my floor," Mama cried. "Please take off your overcoats before the hall becomes a lake."

The man slapped his forehead with his palm, loped to the door, and touched the mezuzah. Anya's stomach knotted as she realized she had forgotten to pay proper tribute to the little prayer box when she got home with Kisa this afternoon.

Papa swept the air in front of him with his arm, like a butler did when dignitaries make grand entrances. "Meet Mr. Daniel Benatar and his son, Gabriel Benatar. I found them at the Cornucopia Tea House on Monday. Daniel was oblivious to the danger. I figured he must have arrived very recently and no one had divulged 'rule number one' for staying alive in Shanghai."

Mama rolled her eyes. Georgi jumped up and down in anticipation of one of Papa's exaggerations. The man puckered his lips and whistled for no reason.

"Which of your rules, Papa?" Anya asked.

"Not *my* rule," he chortled. "Common sense rule number one: Don't stare at Pockmarked Huang! His thugs had been streaming in during tea time to take bribes at the back table. I leaned over to Daniel and warned him to lower his eyes unless he wanted his tall, dark, and handsome son recruited against his will by the Green Gang."

Papa had been sitting in the same room as the Green Gang!

At Anya's pajama party the month before, Sara Tukachinsky said she overheard her parents talking about Shanghai's mafia. They were murderers, opium dealers, kidnappers of heiresses. "Stay away," they said, "from the Green Gang's office on the top floor of the amusement palace, Great World." Each time the wind rustled the bamboo chimes that night, Anya imagined it was the sound of men dressed in green stalking the girls. She had trained one eye on the window throughout the night until Aurora, the goddess of dawn, arrived.

Gabriel's face was handsome. His hair was long, almost touching his shoulders. Compared to the crew cuts of boys in bowling club, Gabriel's hair was dramatic. He looked to be fifteen or sixteen.

"Where is your kitchen, Mrs. Stella Bella?" Mr. Benatar asked, bowing to Mama. He pecked Mama's hand with his lips, then sniffed the air and waved the family to follow him toward the aroma of frying onions.

Tucked into one of his armpits was a bottle of wine and under the other, a paper package that he identified as *Polpettone di Tacchino*. He set both on the cluttered counter next to a wire mesh bowl piled with beet and carrot tops.

"I made this ancient dish in my kitchen this morning." He loosened the string. The paper crinkled and fell away from the turkey loaf. Tapping his temples, he said, "My nonna's box of recipes is stored right here." Then he emptied the contents of his trouser pocket: a wad of paper money, a jar of small black shriveled balls floating in oil, and a chain holding more keys than there were doors for.

"Didn't your nonna teach you it's a bad omen to put your keys on the kitchen table?" Babushka said, tugging the ends of her kerchief tighter. Anya flinched at Babushka's tactlessness.

Mr. Benatar scooped the keys and money into his hand and stuffed them back in his pocket. Instead of acting the way Dedushka would have—like a young boy who had been reprimanded by his favorite teacher—he flashed a charming smile at Babushka and then sliced the end off the loaf. He diced it into six equal portions, and placed one cube in Papa's mouth.

"*Nu?* Is it good or not?" Babushka asked.

Papa pondered the ceiling as he chewed and chewed, then swallowed and said, "Manna."

"What is manna?" Gabriel asked, followed by his father's question, "You eat horse meat?"

"Ha. Ha. Good joke," Georgi said.

"I'm confused." Anya said. "What the heck does manna have to do with horses? This conversation makes no sense."

Papa said, "Gabriel, you are welcome to look up the meaning of manna in the Book of Exodus. But to save you time, I'll paraphrase. God fed the Israelites manna for forty years after they escaped from Egypt. Each morning, he rained down manna on the desert of Zin, covering the sand with white grains that tasted like whatever a person craved—shish kebab, kippered herring, grapes, vanilla cake."

"Chocolate cherries," Georgi interrupted.

"Yes, *sinichka*, chocolate-covered caramels and shortbread, and matzoh, too. It was a miracle."

"Strudel with flaky crust," Anya said.

"*Dolce*." Gabriel grinned. "And ciabatta slathered with butter."

Dolce. Dol-chay. The word rolled off his tongue with a sound that hinted at its meaning: sweet.

"Kugel," Anya said, returning Gabriel's smile. "Wait till you try Li Mei's authentic Chinese recipe."

"Spaghetti and meatballs," Gabriel countered. "Heaped with grated pecorino romano. So much cheese, it buries the noodles."

"I vote for Benatar's *polpettone*," Papa said, eyeing the turkey loaf.

"I accept your compliments," Mr. Benatar said. "And about the horse meat . . . don't you follow the races? Manna is the name of one of the winningest horses in history. He won both the Two Guineas race and the English Derby a dozen years ago."

Papa shook his head and Anya blurted, "Don't get him started—"

"Gambling is for *schlimazels*. Those fools at the Canidrome Race Course are throwing away good money on greyhound bets that should go to feed the poor."

Mr. Benatar didn't comment on Papa's position on gamblers. He held a cube of the loaf up to Anya's mouth as a parent would to a toddler. "Anya, your turn!"

She was hungry as a hog, having missed the arrival at five o'clock of the bean cake man. And because she was fetching soy milk for Kisa during afternoon *chai*, both the tea and the *zakuskas* were devoured by the time she returned. Georgi probably went wild eating up her share of the hors d'oeuvres.

Hungry as she was, sticking out her tongue in front of a boy who made her heart thump a little faster mortified her.

She sniffed the meat and detected nutmeg, and another spice she didn't recognize. "What are the green pieces? Not mold, I hope."

"I don't like chopped pistachios either," Gabriel said, shaking his head and grinning.

Anya gobbled the turkey loaf. "Pretty good for foreign food," she said. "May I have Georgi's share since he didn't save even one tea cake for me?"

Mr. Benatar beamed. He licked his fingers and twisted off the lid from the jar. "Serve the rest of my *polpettone* tomorrow topped with sliced hard-boiled eggs and these *poco* olives from my groves in Riomaggiore." Mr. Benatar whistled at the food like it was a beautiful girl. "This is *my* manna—little oriola olives, the nectar of the Italian Riviera. And I am single-handedly planning an olive invasion of Shanghai. When I read in *The Shanghai Evening Post and Mercury* that it is this city's destiny to become the 'permanent emporium of trade' with Western Europe, in fact every nation worldwide, I determined my humble Fratelli Benatar must aid in this objective."

"Well-mannered men do not whistle indoors," Babushka admonished. "Or brag."

"Forgive my mother, Benatar, she has not adjusted to life in Shanghai," said Mama.

"What is this Benatar business? Please call me Daniel."

"I couldn't." Mama reddened.

Anya studied her mother who was flushed like a nervous bride. She seemed to blossom under Mr. Benatar's gaze. *Why is she pretending to admire the olive branch on the jar's label?*

Mr. Benatar pulled another jar of olives from his other pocket. "For your pantry, Bella."

eleven

Loi Mei rang the dinner bell. Georgi was first to the dining room. Anya lifted the handkerchiefs covering the *challot* and sniffed the braided loaves of egg bread. The crust was still steaming. She raised her eyelids and inhaled to demonstrate how much she loved challah. Gabriel nodded at her and they both blushed.

"Put that cover down," Papa said. "You don't want the challah to get jealous of the wine while it waits to receive the last blessing, do you?"

Why is Gabriel staring at me?

The black curls at Gabriel's shoulders begged Anya's finger to twirl one or two. Did he have a big lump in his throat, too? Maybe he'd choose her as his partner tonight when they played cards after dinner.

Papa poured four ounces of blackberry wine in the silver *kiddush* cup and lifted it in his right hand. "*Sav-rei ma-ra-nan.*" He passed the cup to his left hand and then back to the palm of his right, lowering it until it was exactly nine inches above the table. This was his cue to Georgi to recite the first blessing with him, a privilege saved for boys.

Anya mouthed along anyway "Blessed are You, Lord, our God, King of the Universe, who creates the fruit of the vine."

Papa drank half the wine and poured the remaining portion into six glasses. The family sipped their wine as he poured water from the pitcher over the tops and bottoms of, first his right, then his left hand, three times into the silver basin. Dedushka and Georgi mirrored him, and together they chanted the blessing for washing hands.

On the eve of Shabbat, Anya always looked forward to Saturday, to reading and playing with her canaries. Not tonight. She drummed her fingers to the silent tune of her scales exercises, right to left, left to right, eighteen times, while Papa recited. Mama shot her the stop-squirming look. Anya's mind drifted to Kisa. Had she pooped on Li Mei's bed? Where was Kisa's mother? Was she tormented by abandoning her child? Was she remorseful? Anya's head pounded.

How unfair that men decide the fate of girls! What a horrible rule that wives and girls belong to their husbands' clans and because of this so many Chinese girls die. In ancient Egypt, Pharaoh ordered his soldiers to drown Jewish boys in the Nile River and he let the girls live. How ironic!

When Papa finally said amen, Mr. Benatar blurted, "My Lord, three blessings in less than five minutes."

Papa held his finger up to his mouth and said, "Shhhh."

"We're not allowed to talk between hand-washing and eating the challah. Papa calls this a 'wholly holy moment,'" Anya whispered in his ear.

"But why didn't he wash up in the bathroom before dinner?"

"The water that comes out of a faucet isn't *mayim chayim*, living water. Shhhh."

The male Rosens wiped their hands dry with the embroidered linen cloth Mama saved for Shabbat. Papa and Georgi lifted the two *challot* and placed them side by side for the *hamotzi*. Mr. Benatar and Gabriel bowed their heads and gestured with their hands across and up and down their chests. Papa and Dedushka pretended not to notice.

Mama cringed and Babushka started to reprimand them but Anya interrupted her, "In Italy you add hand motions to the blessing over the bread?" Anya asked Gabriel.

"I was crossing myself in the Name of the Father, the Son, and the Holy Ghost," Gabriel replied.

"Is your Holy Ghost hungry?"

Gabriel tilted his head and made a question mark with his eyes.

"When the moon rises, I'll show you what I'm talking about," Anya said.

Papa tore challah from the first loaf and passed the pieces around the table.

"Dip your bread in the salt water." Anya pointed to the miniature bowl beside Gabriel's and Mr. Benatar's bread plates. Babushka had discovered stacks of the cut crystal salt bowls for sale "at a price that suited her purse" in the Old City but she lied to Mama when she and Anya walked in the door that day, and said she bought the bowls at Bik's on Rue de Cardinal Mercier—the proper place for ladies to purchase china and crystal.

Mr. Benatar touched the tip of his tongue to the piece of bread and asked, "Is Jewish bread made without salt?"

"We dip challah in salt," Papa explained, "to symbolize our eternal covenant with God. And salt makes food tastier, like this moment at our Shabbat table with you and your son, our new friends."

Babushka gulped the last ounce of fruit wine, licked her lips again, and eyed the carafe Papa placed out of her reach. This was how Papa and Dedushka limited her to two glasses.

"Anya. Georgi. Come stand next to me," Papa said, inspecting them as they walked towards him.

Sunday through Thursday, Papa didn't care if his children had messy hair, dirty faces, or holey clothes. But on Shabbat, Papa expected his family to dress up. Otherwise the next Shabbat would be full of trouble.

"Daniel, I am about to say the blessing for the children. I would like to invite Gabriel to join, if you will give your permission."

Mr. Benatar nodded. "Gabriel, go ahead. Go."

Gabriel strolled to the spot next to Anya but Georgi nabbed his sleeve and pulled him to his side. "Stand here. There's a separate blessing for boys."

"I am the oldest," Anya said to Papa.

"You won't let me forget it, will you?" Papa placed his hands above Anya's ears and blessed her, then whispered in her ear, "May God bless your Kisa and protect her, too. Don't worry. I checked before dinner, and she was sleeping peacefully. We both know that Li Mei's Mah-mee will take excellent care of her."

"Speak up, Joshua," said Mr. Benatar. "I cannot hear *sotto voce*."

"Never mind, Daniel. This is between my daughter and me."

The many blessings chanted, Mama directed the guests to their spots at the table. Next to each wineglass was a place card handwritten by Papa. Anya pulled her chair out and was lowering into her seat when Babushka screamed, "Anya, for God's sake, don't sit there!" She turned to Mama and shrieked, "You know better than to seat an unmarried girl at the corner of the table. She will not marry if she sits there." She punctuated "amen" with both pointer fingers aimed at Gabriel.

"Mamochka, please," Mama said, "no superstitions at the Shabbat table."

"She is just a child," Dedushka added. "She is allowed to sit at the corner as long as she is too young to marry for at least seven years."

"I want to sit here. I'm not planning a wedding," Anya said, blushing.

"Pshaw, Anya. Of course, you will marry," Babushka said, "but not until you've finished your voice training and toured Europe with the New York Opera. At least seven to ten years before you can find a husband."

"I know! I know! I am Anya Rosen, daughter of Stella Orjich. *Bat kol.* Anya with the voice of an angel, next in line to be a *virtuosa* like my mother," Anya blurted from embarrassment, then, no sooner, wished she could retract the words. Her cheeks itched and her belly grumbled so loudly, Gabriel must have heard. She rubbed her belly under the table to get the painful cramp to move along her intestines. She excused herself and walked around the table, heading for the bathroom. Her chin itched and the itch moved ahead of her scratching finger to her lower lip.

Babushka wagged her finger. "Old Jewish saying: If your lips itch, you'll kiss someone soon. Amen."

If I am lucky, this is a mosquito bite and I will die of malaria, the easy way out of dinner with this crazy family.

Big Ching chimed eight o'clock. Mo-chou and Li Mei carried in platters heaped with buckwheat *piroshki*, roast chicken, dill potatoes, noodle kugel, *tzimmes*, and *pierogi*. Anya placed a pair of *quai-tse* between Gabriel's thumb, index, and middle fingers and demonstrated how to pick up shreds of honey-sweetened carrots using chopsticks. She repeated the rules Li Mei taught her: "Don't collide with your neighbor's chopsticks. Never point one at a human being. Don't drum the tips on the table unless you're a beggar. Never, ever, stand the stick upright in your rice or bad luck will befall the household."

"I am in heaven. *Piu*," Mr. Benatar said as he chewed a bite of kugel with chipmunk cheeks, gesturing to the ceiling, then popping another bite into his already full mouth.

Georgi whispered to Anya, "Did he just say 'pee-yew'?"

"*Piu* means 'more,'" Gabriel snickered.

"I'd like to make my nonna's noodle pie for the Rosens. Riomaggiore is the perfect climate for durum wheat to grow, the most important ingredient of real Italian noodles, which I import, of course."

"Pasta was not invented by the Italians, with all due respect, Mr. Benatar. The ancient Talmud documents dried noodles called *itriyah*," said Dedushka.

"I won't argue with you, sir. But I can assure you it was an

Italian who invented the first pasta-maker. King Ferdinand II of Naples didn't approve of kneading pasta dough with the feet, so he hired an engineer to solve the problem."

"The Chinese have been eating noodles made from millet for five thousand years," Li Mei said.

"Lovely Li Mei, you are *ostinato*. Joshua, you are surrounded by a quartet of obstinate women. I will remember this important trivia from the mouth of an authentic Chinese cook when I set out to impress new Chinese customers. Thanks to you, I will carve a larger share of the Chinese melon."

"Melons aren't Chinese, are they?" Georgi said.

"A poetic figure of speech about capitalists, son. The harder we work in our businesses, the more Chinese money we will put in our pockets. That's what carving the melon means."

"Fortunately, Daniel, you have chosen a country where very little of that Chinese money will leave your pocket when it's time to pay your domestic expenses. Every man can live grandly here because money stretches much further than in Europe. We've managed to fill three stories with carved French furniture. We own a telephone in its own wall nook. Our bathrooms are plumbed with plenty of hot water to fill the marble bathtubs. I don't mean to brag—I am so grateful—but best of all these amenities is our icebox. And we can even afford a houseful of servants. Until your wife joins you, you and Gabriel shouldn't need more than a Number One boy who you will pay fifty dollars per month—"

"I am no longer married to Gabriel's mother." Mr. Benatar announced this shocking information as matter-of-factly as a conductor reporting the train had just departed the station.

"Forgive me for asking, but I am curious. What happened?" Papa said.

"There are no secrets amongst friends. Julia petitioned to annul our marriage soon after Gabriel was born. My sister, Domenica, and I were raised Catholic—"

Babushka gasped twice and opened her mouth, but before she could derail Mr. Benatar's story, Dedushka said, "Silence!"

"We married in the Roman Catholic church. Thirteen years ago, when my poppa was on his deathbed, he asked me to fetch the Bible from his nightstand and turn to the first half, the Hebrew portion. He said, 'Follow the Torah and pray for Israel. You are a chosen one. We are Jewish.'

"That was my bar mitzvah. It was also the requiem of my marriage. Julia petitioned the Vatican the very next day. Gabriel lived with his mother until it was time to learn his Torah portion for his bar mitzvah."

"You are a Crypto-Jew," Papa said in amazement.

What's so stunning about that? Anya wondered. She wanted to tell the adults to close their mouths or an entire mosquito family would hatch from the eggs.

"I am ashamed to admit my father hid our Judaism. He did it to protect his family. Even in our peaceful village, the Christian neighbors blamed the Jews for burglaries, murders, financial problems, even the drought. Each time a new man joined the police department, it was only a matter of days before he banged on our front door."

"But if you were pretending to be Catholic—" Anya said.

"—The candle glow through our closed curtains alerted

him, perhaps. The policeman would line us up in the foyer and inspect our jewelry for the Star of David and our cabinets and closets for any telltale sign of Judaism. Finding nothing, he would huff out the door. Nonna and Mamma rushed around the rooms, returning strewn clothing to drawers, foodstuffs to the pantry, and books to the library shelves. *Mio padre's* face was always sad after a visit from the Jewcatchers, but he didn't allow us to blow out the candles. Nonna set them under the table and we'd go up to bed early."

"You were lucky your house didn't burn to the ground," Mama said.

Mr. Benatar placed his palms together in a gesture of prayer and pointed his fingertips at Papa. "Enough morose conversation. I didn't mean to change the mood of the evening. Tell me more, please, about the staff I will need to help raise my boy."

Papa continued his list. "There's more you need to know about Number One boy's pay: In addition to his salary, you give him a squeeze of five percent on all the supplies he buys for you, and a *cumshaw*."

Mama fidgeted at the talk of money at Shabbat.

"*Cumshaw?*"

"Tip. You will also need one or two house coolies at eighteen dollars each, a wash and *sew-sew* amah at twenty dollars. I pay our gardeners twenty each—"

"Papi, will we hire a chauffeur?" Gabriel asked. "I'll need rides from school to tennis practice."

"Where are you going to school?" Anya asked him.

"The Shanghai Jewish School. Is that your school?"

Anya nodded. "Watch out for Headmistress Perry. She's on a rampage to make sure her students get admitted to elite British universities."

"I don't approve of your religion teacher," Babushka said.

Anya explained, "Mr. Brown is our teacher *and* the rabbi of Ohel Rachel and he's"—Anya drummed on the table for a buildup of suspense—"Sephardic."

"Anya! One more show of disrespect to your grandmother and you will excuse yourself from this table," Papa said. "Chen is the highest-paid member of my staff, well worth the sixty dollars I pay him. Be very careful when you hire, though. Communist posers have infiltrated the city. Don't get caught by the Nationalists for harboring one of Sun Yat-sen's spies."

"And where do I find my own Li Mei?" Mr. Benatar quipped.

"We are very fortunate. Li Mei's mother, Jia Li, provided her girl with apprenticeships in Indian, Russian, and French kitchens for her eventual employment with one of the immigrant families. She also rigorously tutored her in English and a bit of Russian. Li Mei can recite hundreds of poems from memory. I pay her thirty-five."

"Giselle has *two* cooks," Anya said.

"Who's Giselle?" Gabriel asked, and tore the rest of the skin off his drumstick with his teeth.

"She's my best friend and lives right next door. You'd like her. She's from Germany, but acts Australian."

Anya didn't have to explain what she meant to Gabriel. It was as though he understood the way she looked at the world. Another boy would have thought she was insulting Germans.

"Do Aussies play cards? Can we call and invite her to play a game with us after dinner?" Gabriel added. "I want to meet your friends."

Anya's mood soared and suddenly she hoped the meal would go on and on. "Mr. Lindberg hasn't bought a phone yet, and we can't knock on her door. She's not allowed to have visitors after Shabbat begins. Are you free on Sunday?"

Gabriel nodded his head with a wide smile on his face. "I'm free for my first friends in China!"

Anya had never before made a friend of a boy. He was easy to talk to. She wasn't embarrassed to tell him the story of Papa bringing her the canaries so she wouldn't be so lonely for Luba, Angelica, and Lily. Gabriel didn't know much about Amelia Earhart's disappearance, but perked up and listened to every word when she related an amazing coincidence: that the plane Amelia's husband bought her was called an Electra. The star, Electra, one of the seven Pleiades, was referred to as "the Lost Pleiad." Amelia Earhart was lost in a plane named after a lost star!

Gabriel nodded his head. His eyes were curious. He gulped the rest of his ice water and politely asked Mo-chou for a refill.

"And there's more!" Georgi added. "Did you know the star Electra purposely left her spot in the sky before the Greek army destroyed Troy? She didn't want to see soldiers burning and tearing up her homeland."

"I did read that star story," Gabriel said. He called out to Mr. Benatar, "Papi, I'm glad we left Italy before the Nazis burned down our olive trees."

Gabriel didn't look away like most boys. He didn't hide the

tear in his eye when he talked about the possibility of losing his home. He spoke his mind. He didn't appear to care whether or not he impressed her.

I like him.

"Son, we won't lose our land," Mr. Benatar said with urgency in his voice.

This was the first time since Anya met the man that he sounded anxious.

"From your lips to God's ears," Babushka said.

"Amen," the whole group affirmed at the same time, and their whoops and giggles mixed together into one big hilarity.

After the laughter died down, Gabriel asked Anya, "How many months before you felt Chinese?"

"I still miss Odessa every day. I'll never be Chinese. But I'm beginning to understand Mandarin and some pidgin English, and I love bean cakes."

After mashing carrots into her uneaten potatoes and chicken, Anya set her fork down with a clank. Sitting in this chair next to Gabriel was a terrific way to spend Shabbat, but she still didn't have much of an appetite. Wasn't she wasting time at a fancy meal when a child with no future was motherless in her basement? Had she known she was frowning and had she plastered on a fake smile just then, Babushka might have stayed out of her pounding head.

"What's with the sour puss?" she asked. "You didn't eat your chicken *baguette*."

"Mamochka, you're wixing your mords again," Papa quipped.

"Rosengartner, she is confused, but not the way you think.

Baguette is also a musical term in French—*baguette de bois*—wooden drumstick. She means the chicken, not a loaf of bread," Mama corrected Papa, then addressed Babushka in a whisper, "No more wine."

"I gave my baguette to Gabriel since he's the guest," Anya said, wishing she could disappear like Electra.

"When I was your age, Anya," Mama said, "Dedushka left for the war. On Shabbat, all Babushka served my older sisters and I was half a bowl of cabbage soup with a few measly fish scraps floating on top. The czar rationed one loaf of green pea bread per family. The bread line Mamochka made me wait in for hours stretched a mile down Boulevard Gavannaia."

"The grape harvest was ruined, so there wasn't a bottle of wine available," Babushka added. "We drank *kvass*, a sour drink made from fermented barley. I begged in front of the Winter Palace with Lara on my lap, hoping one of the princesses would take pity."

"My hungry belly ached all the time, especially in the morning," Mama said.

"Georgi, cut the potato in half, not such big bites." Babushka shot Georgi her look that meant, "Push one more beet with your mama's sterling silver knife off the edge of your plate to hide it, Buster, and you will go to your room without a bite of dessert."

"Listen to your grandmother. She knows what's best," Papa added.

"If you grow any more blubber on that belly," Babushka warned Georgi, "your mother will send you to Anya's ballet class in a chiffon tutu."

"Mamochka, I would never subject Georgi to that. Don't be cruel."

Dedushka sucked the marrow out of the end of a chicken wing. "Greed is like lust," he said. "It destroys a man." He wiped the grease off the edges of his mouth with the one corner of his napkin not covered with drops of sauce.

"Be quiet, old *fortz*," Babushka said.

Papa, why do you allow her to call Dedushka names at the Shabbat table? And in front of guests!

Georgi slammed out of his chair.

"Every single meal someone tells me something else I can't eat. Don't eat meat at the same meal with dairy foods. Don't eat sweets because you're too fat. Don't eat limbs of animals that died of natural causes or died in a fight with another animal—" Georgi coughed, cleared his throat, coughed again, and sputtered.

He is choking! Anya jumped up to help Mr. Benatar slap Georgi's back. On the fourth try, a half-chewed piece of challah projected over the table and landed on Babushka's lap.

"Shah!"

"Don't eat winged, swarming insects or creeping bugs," Georgi continued, clearing his throat. He threw his napkin on the floor.

"Papa, do something about his temper!" Anya said, stooping to pick up the crumpled napkin and fold it.

"Don't start," Mama said, pointing her finger at Georgi, and then Anya.

"Enough, son. You may not be rebellious against the voice of your mother. You must honor your father *and* your mother."

Georgi didn't acknowledge Papa's warning. He sprinted from the room and clambered up the stairs.

Anya sighed and returned to her seat. *The little squirt is the precious son.*

Gabriel offered Anya the fruit bowl. While he held it for her, she squeezed each peach. Once she found the ripest one, she polished off the fuzz with her napkin. She thought about how Gabriel's presence at the table made her nervous and calm at the same time. During the main course, he had dipped the edge of his napkin in his glass of ice water after a julienne of carrot dropped from Anya's chopstick and spotted the tablecloth. He had scrubbed the orange stain until it lightened, with concentration and care, as though he was protecting her from harm.

How was it possible to want the butterflies in her stomach to stay, not fly away? She found herself leaning toward him while they talked. When their hands touched while reaching for another hunk of challah, he didn't pull away.

This peach is so delicious. Dolce. Dolce.

twelve

as it possible to find a mother who didn't want anyone to find her? Were there signs on a woman's body that proved she had recently given birth? Anya couldn't just approach any Chinese woman tomorrow and ask, "Excuse me, did you lose your daughter in my alley?" She wondered where to start her search.

As Mo-chou cleared the dinner dishes, Anya excused herself to go to the bathroom again. Gabriel stared at her as she slipped from her seat, but no one followed her down the stairs. Mama would think she had primped, then gone to reprimand Georgi and bring him back in tow.

She tapped on Dandan's door with her fingernail.

"Who is it?" a nervous voice squeaked.

"Let me in. It's Anya."

"I can't, Miss Ani-ah. Li Mei told me not even to *crack* open this door."

"Pretend there's a fire in the kitchen and you have to escape."

The door whipped open. Dandan yanked Anya into the room. "Just a quick look, if you want your blouses starched the way you like them."

Anya reached into the basket cradle and kissed Kisa's tiny hand. The walls of the room shuddered from the wind, but the air smelled cozy. The candles gave the room the light of a lullaby.

"Remember to change Kisa's nappy. And give her plenty to drink, okay?"

Dandan said, "Um-hhm."

Kisa's eyes opened and she gurgled. *Why can't Kisa grow up with our new baby?*

"Please go now, Missy!"

Satisfied that Dandan was taking plenty good care of her, Anya tiptoed out. Before she returned to her seat in the dining room, she would let Mama's temper cool a bit longer.

She sailed up three flights of steps to her bedroom, shut the door, and jumped onto her bed. She stomped her pillows— once, twice, again and again, one stomp for each mean word, angry expression, abandoned girl, hungry beggar, lost pilot who ever lived. Once she began, she found reason after reason to stomp. Were Georgi's ears plastered on the other side listening, or was he busy with his soldiers acting out a battle?

Anya dived under the cotton sheets down to the corner tuck, which smelled like fresh rain. Big Ching was in the middle of a chime. Nine o'clock already? Almost time for dessert, and then cards. She closed her eyes and lay in the cool peace for a few moments more.

What are children born for? she pondered.

A few moments passed and she still hadn't settled on an answer when she realized she had missed the birds' feeding time by almost four hours. Normally, she was as strict as a stopwatch about their schedule, beginning each day at six A.M. Breakfast was a blend of millet, flax seed, carrots, and apple slices. At noon, she refilled the water bowl, sprayed cool mist on their heads and wings, and changed their newspaper. At five thirty sharp, it was supper time. When the sun went down, she covered their cages with the new shawl embroidered with Siamese cats that Li Mei had given her for her birthday. Every Saturday at nine A.M., Anya put the birds in their small cages and walked them to French Park on Route Voyron, where they met Giselle and her parrot with a German accent, Eliza. On the first day of each month, she scrubbed the cages with a dilution of bleach and potassium permanganate in warm water.

Tonight, Anya didn't replace yesterday's *Shanghai Evening Post and Mercury* on the cage bottom, despite the green splat soiling Papa's article about Generalissimo Chiang Kai-shek. She fed the birds and, before they had finished, draped the shawl over the birdcage.

"*Bon soir, mon pauvre petit poulets.*"

Giselle thought it was hilarious that some nights, she called her canaries poor little chickens, other nights, ducks. It depended on the birds' moods. *Canard* sounded more like canary than *poulet*, but Pidge didn't like it when Anya called him a duck.

Fifteen minutes later, Anya and Georgi bumped into each other in the hallway. Anya sniffed the air and licked her lips at the smell of hot peach strudel, her favorite Shabbat dessert.

"Race you," she said, and sped by him before he could drape his chunky leg over the banister. She skidded to a stop at the dining room entrance as Georgi reached the bottom newel post. "One day, you'll catch up with your superior sister."

They slipped into their seats and picked up their forks in unison to take their first bite of strudel.

Gabriel whispered, "I hoped you'd come down to play cards."

Anya blushed. "Do you know how to play Six Tigers?" she asked.

"You mean Six Points?"

"You are in China. We call it Six Tigers here," Anya corrected him. She pushed her chin forward like Mama did when she argued with Papa.

The old copper samovar, passed down through several generations of Rosengartners, sputtered. Li Mei poured a half cup of concentrated tea into Papa's *potstikani* from the pot on top of the tea-maker, then added boiling water from the spigot. Papa still drank his tea in the old style, slurping through a sugar cube held between his front teeth.

Anya's slice of strudel was larger than Georgi's and Gabriel's. She shoveled in bites she dipped in a vanilla ice cream moat. Babushka slid her finger through the pool of melted ice cream on Dedushka's plate.

"No more sweets for you, Chaim."

"Leave me be," Dedushka said.

"May the Lord help you if Dr. Smolenski sees how big your belly has grown. You'll have another heart attack. God forbid."

Anya was weary of the bickering at every meal, even dessert. She played her block-out-the-sound game. She silently recited, as fast as she could, the thirty-nine categories of work that were forbidden on Shabbat, starting with no hitting with a hammer, and ending with no extinguishing a fire.

"Papa, a Japanese soldier whacked a Chinese man's head with his rifle today," Georgi cried, bringing Anya's attention back to dinner.

Papa kneaded his knuckles. "When Japanese soldiers are hurt or killed, General Sugiyama punishes the Chinese for the aggression. China's loyalists call the violence 'the War to Resist the Japanese.' I predict this is the beginning of a second world war."

"Why do people kill? Can't they settle their differences with diplomacy? Why did we come here, Papi?" Gabriel asked.

"I want to move to New York before Shanghai burns to the ground," Anya said.

Papa's face turned red, and he slapped a hand on the table. "We're not leaving a land where we are finally free. We will stay, God willing, until the Chinese kick us out."

The day they debarked the ship in Shanghai, Papa had kneeled and kissed the stones on the ground, his *tallus* fringe sweeping the muddy snow. He would have rolled in the dust, had Mama and Babushka not frowned with a you-better-not expression. Papa loved it here.

"Is it your opinion, Joshua, that the Chinese will retain control of Shanghai, including the foreign concessions?" Mr. Benatar asked.

"This is my greatest wish! But any man who believes *that* doesn't understand how devious the Japanese are. Recently, they bombed Nankai University in Tientsin because they claimed it was a center of anti-Japanese activities. But the real reason was retaliation. Two of the university president's sons are aviators with the Chinese Air Corps."

Papa lifted his almost empty wine goblet and looked at Anya. "I've been waiting for the right time to make an announcement. This is as good as any."

The chattering and eating stopped.

Anya felt her face flush warm, then cold. *It's about time Papa tells Mama the plans we've kept secret for weeks.*

"My editor, Cornelius van der Starr, offered me a promotion and a raise in pay."

Anya sighed with disappointment. *Once and for all, can't we tell Mama I am quitting my lessons with Maestro?* But she clapped for Papa and rose her glass high to clink with the others.

Dedushka hooted, "Mazel tov, Joshua. Our fortunes are turning." He burst from his chair and walked with an uncharacteristic spring in his step over to Papa. Mr. Benatar joined him and, as if on cue, both men clapped Papa on the back.

"Good luck, my friend," Mr. Benatar said.

"What is your new title, may I ask?" Mama said.

"I am the war correspondent. For the time being, I will cover day-to-day activities in Shanghai. But I have agreed to travel where needed. Van der Starr will send me upriver where Japanese troops are swelling next month. Around Nanjing."

"Such dangerous work, Joshua," said Babushka, shaking her head. "Do you have a death wish?"

"No, Mamochka, of course not. It is my duty to provide well

for my family. With a bun in the oven, I cannot refuse better pay." Papa swilled the wine in his glass and then raised his hands in the air like a rabbi.

Maybe tomorrow, we'll tell Mama. And if Mama took the news badly, Anya could always flee like He Xian-Gu did. She was the Immortal who disappeared on her dreaded wedding day and climbed Luofu Mountain to study Taoism instead of marry. This story Li Mei had told her about a courageous girl making her own decisions—making her own way—reassured her. He Xian-Gu eventually became an Immortal after a deity revealed how to grind mica into powder and consume a spoonful. Now, the tale goes, she lives in mountains where it's forever summer, bowls are never empty of rice, and no one feels pain.

The family finished drinking their tea, but only Papa and Dedushka dared slurp like Jia Li had taught them soon after they arrived from Odessa. She had visited her daughter at teatime and instructed, "Make a little noise. Show your appreciation. Leave a shallow pool at the bottom of the cup, so Li Mei will know you are finished."

The last flake of crust had disappeared from Dedushka's plate, and Papa lead the *birkat hamazon*, grace after meals.

"Daniel, please join me in the parlor for cocktails—I'm serving my specialty, sherry flips—and a game of cards. Gabriel may take the third seat at the game table. Stella refuses to play, and Chaim has heartburn, so I asked Li Mei to play at the fourth seat."

"She is dressed like a boat woman," Mama whispered, horrified. "Li Mei may not enter the formal rooms of my home in that shapeless dress."

"Mama! Li Mei might hear you," Anya pleaded. "I can lend her one of my dresses."

"Good idea, Anya," Papa said. "You two are about the same size. Fetch her from the kitchen and take her upstairs. Quickly."

Anya could feel Mama's eyes on her back as she and Li Mei flew up the grand staircase.

Upstairs in Anya's room, Li Mei rubbed her hand over a *crepe-de-chine* dress embroidered with a Russian peasant design. "This *schmata* is perfect for a cook."

Sometimes Li Mei took her limited knowledge of Yiddish a bit too far. But tonight her comparison of the most expensive couture dress in her closet to a rag was hilarious.

"Don't let Mama hear you calling my new Coco Chanel dress a *schmata*."

The dress was a little too loose on Li Mei and perhaps too long—skimming her ankle bones instead of her calves. But the sea green color complemented her skin tone beautifully and when Li Mei let her long hair out of her bun and it swished down her back, Anya knew why Jules considered her the loveliest girl in Shanghai.

"This is much better than a *qipao*," Li Mei said with relief. "I can bend my elbows. It is loose enough for my skin to feel the air. I hope this satisfies Madame and she stops fighting with your papa."

"Before China, Mama and Papa never argued!" Anya said.

"There isn't a matchmaker in Asia who would have betrothed your mother to your father. What an unfortunate match."

"My mama picked her own husband without a matchmaker. Only old-fashioned Jews use a *yenta*."

"The animals presiding over your parents' birth hours are enemies. Madame Stella is a tiger and Master Josh is a serpent. Your parents' elements aren't harmonious either."

"What element is Mama?"

"Fire, of course."

"So Papa is water."

"Smart, Missy." Li Mei grabbed Anya's hand and pulled her into the hallway.

By the time Li Mei took her seat at the card table, Papa had served Mr. Benatar his second after-dinner drink. Mama and Georgi sat on the settee closest to Mr. Benatar's chair. Dedushka and Babushka snored in unison on the couch near Papa's seat. Anya snuck a stare at Gabriel as Mr. Benatar snapped the cards from the shuffled deck, and dealt twelve cards each to the three players, laying them down on the mahogany surface.

Why is Mama staring at Mr. Benatar's hands? His manly fingers and clean nails contrasted with Papa's stubby, ink-stained fingers and blotchy knuckles.

They played a few rounds before Mr. Benatar spread five cards like a peacock tail and laid five aces face up.

"Five tigers emerge from the mountains," Li Mei shouted, jumping from her seat and toppling her chair.

Mr. Benatar slapped his palms on his thighs in a drum roll.

The four played round after round of Six Tigers and Papa kept score. The third time he guffawed louder than he had since the spring, Mama ruined the happy mood.

"You sound like a hyena, Rosen," Mama said.

Poor Papa. Why does he let Mama slap him with her words?

"Stella, why do you call Joshua by his last name?" Mr. Benatar asked.

"In our country, first names are saved for private conversations between a husband and his wife," Papa answered. "Stella, isn't it time we changed our old ways? We're in Shanghai now and one day we will live in America. You have my permission to call me Joshua."

"Not as long as I'm alive," Dedushka said, and cleared his throat noisily.

When she married, if she married, Anya planned to be a loving wife and call her husband by his first name. Bobby. Or Gabriel.

At half past ten, the game ended. Mr. Benatar shook hands with Papa. "Thank you, Joshua. This was a perfect cure for Gabriel's homesickness. And mine."

"Papi, when you were a child, didn't you play cards on Friday nights, too?"

"Yes, we did, son. It was our *intermezzo* between Shabbat dessert and breakfast in the morning."

"*Intermezzo* is not the right word," Mama said. "Card games are not the same thing as light theater."

"Bella, you are *ostinato*, like the rest of them," he said. "Italians often borrow musical terms to express happiness. We played cards as light amusement between very serious bouts of eating."

"Let's finish this party with music." Papa rubbed his hands together. "Daniel, would you like to hear my Stella sing?"

"Yes! A beautiful idea."

Mama nodded like a schoolgirl waiting for a gold star on her forehead for everyone to see.

"Anya, accompany your Mama." Papa nudged her towards the piano.

"How about 'Habanera' from *Carmen*?" Mama said.

If Anya didn't sit on the piano bench *immediatement* and play the grace notes of the Bizet piece, Mama would become grumpy. Gabriel stood next to her and offered to turn the pages of the libretto. Mama waited for the first eight bars, then at the crescendo her voice lifted like a songbird's and filled the gabled room. Mama was Carmen, the Gypsy, teasing the soldiers who were in love with her. She was made for that part. She even looked like a Gypsy. When they used to shop at the Greek bazaar on Krasny Alley, Mama would sail down the red rows of stalls, bargaining with merchants for a new bracelet to add to the collection always clanging around her wrist. At Santsenbakher's Circus, Mama couldn't take her eyes off the Gypsy girls flying on the trapeze to the melody of a mandolin.

Babushka's and Dedushka's jowls quivered and they gazed up at the corners of the ceiling, looking for the angels. Mama's colorful voice gently slid in pitch. If she hadn't left Odessa, opera fans all over the world would be raving about her impressive *portamento*. How awful for her not to follow her childhood dream.

"Brava," Dedushka bellowed.

Mr. Benatar clapped, and said, "*Espressivo*, like Anya's hair. Such expressive curls, especially when you play the piano, young lady."

I never thought my hair had a good personality. Leave it to

Mr. Benatar to turn the major source of my family's insults into a compliment.

"*Bel canto,*" Mr. Benatar coughed into his handkerchief, covering his mouth and wiping his eyes at the same time.

The Italian words were notes of a piano blended with wind. It was as if Mr. Benatar was singing a duet with Mama.

Don't flutter your eyelashes like that . . . Mama.

Papa, do you see?

Stop looking at my mama that way.

Although Anya was supposed to play this part of the melody *pianissimo*—very soft—she played louder, very, very loud, intending with the *fortississimo* to drown out Mama's beautiful singing voice. Then she picked up the pace, playing fast and spirited to force Mama's attention from Mr. Benatar back to Seville and the troubadours. But Mama sang louder. Her voice overpowered the piano, matching Anya's *allegro vivace*, note for note.

Georgi's left ear was pushed against the grille of the radio. He twisted the volume dial with a jerk and the button fell off in his hand.

"Georgi. Mute that radio. Your mother is singing," Papa said.

"You need to hear this," he screamed. "The storm has changed direction and wind speed. A typhoon will hit Shanghai in the middle of the night. Listen—'lock windows and doors. Make sure children are confined to the safest rooms of your home. Remain in a safe place until the danger is over. We will continue to broadcast the changing conditions.'"

"Oh, God, why do you punish us?" Dedushka said, wringing his hands.

"Papachka, calm down," Mama said. "Georgi, turn off the radio this minute. Do you want to kill your grandfather?"

"It is a bad sign when God hides behind a storm to wreak his havoc," Dedushka cried. His cheeks and forehead were dotted like pox with perspiration.

Papa put his hand on Mr. Benatar's shoulder. "It is high tide. The water could rise above the riverbanks, and flood the Bund. You two must stay the night with us, my friend."

"But I don't wish to trouble your family —"

"— no trouble, Danny Benatar," Mama interrupted. "You won't find a car this late in Frenchtown. And we don't drive after Shabbat begins," she said.

Mama rang her bell for Mo-chou and ordered her to place candles and matchboxes throughout the apartment.

"Don't forget to put coasters underneath," Babushka said.

How easily Mama's tune had changed. Suddenly she accepted Papa's rule not to start the car ignition after sunset on Friday. Every rainy Saturday, Mama pleaded with Papa to let Chen drive her to her ladies' luncheons. He would say, "*Nyet*, Stella-chka. It is forbidden to kindle fire on Shabbat. The car's engine burns gasoline and oil. *That* constitutes fire and you know it. How many times do I need to explain to you?"

Mama's face would droop like a sunflower at the end of an Odessa summer, and yet she demanded a ride the next Saturday and the next.

"Change Georgi's bed and his trundle with the Egyptian linens for Mr. Benatar and Gabriel," she continued. "Georgi will sleep on the floor in Dedushka's room tonight."

"Take your radio with you," Anya added, "and don't awaken us at the crack of dawn with a BBC report."

News of the dangerous weather ended the Shabbat celebration. Babushka and Dedushka held Georgi's hand and led him to bed. He looked over his shoulder and stuck his tongue out at Anya and Gabriel.

Mama ushered the Benatars to Georgi's room at eleven o'clock. After Big Ching finished chiming, Papa rushed to prepare for his midnight prayers. Anya slipped into her bedroom but being a girl who couldn't leave well enough alone, she peeked out into the hall before she flipped the light switch. Gabriel wasn't standing at her door as she had secretly hoped.

thirteen

Anya closed her door and climbed into bed. Drops of condensation fell from the air and weighed on the wings of mosquitoes, causing them to dive like helicopters between the tufts of Anya's rug. She rolled from one moist spot on her sheet to another, desperate for a cool patch. The breeze grazed her face and ruffled the fine curls sprouting at her hairline. She pretended Gabriel was touching her hair. *He is on the other side of that wall, asleep in Georgi's bed. Is he thinking about me, too?* She felt guilty thinking about Gabriel when until a few hours ago Bobby Sassoon had consumed her thoughts. There was nothing to feel bad about. Bobby hadn't even kissed her yet. They weren't pinned. She could think about whomever she pleased.

The perfume of jasmine was so strong the blossoms must not have curled into sleep with the rest of the day-blooming flowers. Anya repositioned the fan to blow on her bed. She uncovered her stomach even though Babushka warned that baring skin could result in her death if she should catch a bad cold. *I don't care if the rain floods my room, and the wind blows the furniture out the window. Give me relief from this unbearably hot night!*

Anya's brain was much too crowded to wait until after the end of Shabbat tomorrow to write down her thoughts. So what if writing, even touching her fountain pen, was prohibited until after the *Havdalah* ceremony. Today she had saved a baby and juggled the attention of not one, but two, boys, and during it all she'd hardly thought about Amelia Earhart. Before she could turn in, she'd write the letter to Eleanor Roosevelt she'd been formulating in her mind:

Dear Mrs. Roosevelt:

I am writing to tell you how much I admire you. I think you have loads of courage to take flying lessons. I bet Amelia Earhart is a great instructor. Did she take you up in the air in her yellow Kinner Canary? Did you know tomorrow is her fortieth birthday? Please ask your husband, the President, not to call off the navy search for her plane. My papa, Jake Rosen, war correspondent for *The Shanghai Evening Post and Mercury*, says, "Why not search for one more week since you've already spent four million dollars." If I were in charge of the world, I wouldn't stop searching until we found Amelia Earhart.

Anya dropped the *Book of Moons* on her rug, rolled to the wall, and curled into the shape of a crescent moon. She sang the *Sh'ma* in her prettiest voice, softly to the wall—*Sh'ma Yis'ra'eil Adonai Eloheinu Adonai echad.* Hear, O Israel, the Lord is our God, the Lord is One. *Barukh sheim k'vod malkhuto l'olam va'ed.* Blessed be the Name of His glorious kingdom forever and ever—when the noise of one clap, and then another startled her. She threw off her sheet and went out to the terrace. *Chime. Chime. Chime.* Anya counted to twelve. It was midnight.

Papa believed that his clap sweetened the forces of severity in the world and thus every Shabbat accompanied his midnight prayers with applause. He said he didn't need an alarm clock to awaken at twelve. "The moon is a Jewish timepiece. My body senses the hour, as if angels are whispering, 'Rise' in my ear." Could Papa send Anya's problems away with *clap, clap*: Kisa's mother bows and apologizes for accidentally leaving her daughter on the curb. *Clap, clap.* AMELIA EARHART IS ALIVE AND WELL printed above the fold on the front page of *The Shanghai Evening Post and Mercury. Clap, clap.* The Japanese turn around and retreat to where they belong.

Giselle's house was unusually dark. Mrs. Lindberg often painted at her easel in the sun porch until at least one in the morning. Giselle said her mother was determined to re-create every one of her paintings that used to hang in several galleries in Berlin—until the Nazis hunted down "degenerate" art and burned her canvasses in a street bonfire.

When did the wind stop? The sky sparkled with stars and a cloud scampered over the moon. A nocturne of crickets accompanied the moon glow plaiting light across the terrace.

Is this the eye of the typhoon?

Papa would take credit for changing the storm's course. His prayers were that powerful.

The door to her parents' bedroom was cracked opened. Papa stood by the open window in the lamplight. He stood straight and tall when he prayed. His hunched shoulders disappeared.

Surrounding him were walls covered with oil paintings—two in the rococo style, a Matisse that might be an original, and Mama's portrait hanging over their bed. Papa's suit was draped on the wooden valet. The rest of his wardrobe was stuffed into a large dresser because Mama didn't have room for his things in her walk-in closet. Now that he was an official journalist, he would buy new clothes instead of rotating between his one wool winter suit and two pin-striped summer suits that were identical, except for the shade of gray.

Anya rarely had the opportunity to see inside the room because Mama kept her door closed. *I shouldn't watch.* Papa bent to touch Mama's face and Anya couldn't pull her eyes away. He kissed the black beauty mark the size of a poppy seed on the corner of Mama's eyelid.

"Little *maniki!* I am transfixed by this little nose," he said out loud, kissing the freckles on the tip.

Anya inherited Mama's *maniki.* So why did Natalie Samson and Dora Cravens call her "a large-nosed bottom fish" in front of the composition class her first week in Shanghai? Anya's petite button nose was *not* large or misshapen. Anya had wanted to yell at those girls that day, but had remembered Papa's warning: "Mind your tone with people in powerful positions, such as the Europeans, the Americans, and Mama."

Papa said to Mama, "When you are fast asleep, I can say, *Ya lu blue ti biah,* as often as I want without irritating you."

Ya lu blue ti biah. I love you. Anya didn't run into the room and shake Mama, and ask, "Why do you snap at Papa who loves you this much?" But she wanted to.

As if Mama heard Anya's silent plea, she wrapped her arms

around Papa's neck and touched her mouth to his. Li Mei had told Anya it was a wife's duty to meet her husband in bed once every five days until she reached the age of fifty. *They better not meet right in front of me*, Anya thought.

Papa turned his head suddenly, and looked right at Anya. He put his finger to his lips and gestured for her to leave.

A minute later he appeared in the hallway and followed her to the end. "You *mazik*. Why is my charming daughter sneaking around at midnight?"

"I couldn't fall asleep. The wind was blowing my eyes open. Now it's too quiet."

"It was a noisy bugger tonight, wasn't it? But the typhoon blew over."

"How do you know that, Papa?"

"I heard the wind changing direction."

"Why do you kiss Mama? She humiliated you at dinner."

"The right side of her neck is as smooth as whipping cream and begs for my kisses."

"Ugh, Papa. Stop."

"And I believe the entire purpose of God's creation is to establish *shalom bayit*, harmony between husband and wife. This is why I kiss your mama after I say my prayers. Why stop kissing and loving? I hope I will not live to see the day your mama goes to her grave."

"You sound like Philemon."

"Philip who?"

"Papa. Don't tease. Philemon, husband of Baucis, the old couple who adored each other so much that when Jupiter and

Mercury asked what they wanted as a reward for their hospitality to the gods, they begged to die in each other's arms at the exact same moment."

"Does this have something to do with our linden tree in Odessa?" Papa asked.

"See. You do remember the ending. Why do you tease me about the myths when you like to listen when Mama reads *Bulfinch's*, too?"

"Because the prospect of Mama and I turning into a linden and an oak is not palatable. Dust to dust, that's what Jews believe about the cycle of life and death. Do you know what tree we planted next to the linden in our old front yard?"

She shook her head.

"An oak. I planted both trees as a wedding gift to your mother. You're not the first Rosengartner your mama read *Bulfinch's Mythology* to. Cover to cover!"

"Papa, I bet Philemon and Baucis were Jewish. Remember what they served Jupiter for dessert?"

"I wasn't there. I don't know."

"Papa. Stop." She squeezed his hand. "Apples and wild honey."

"Why does that make them Jewish?"

"Don't we eat apples dipped in honey on Rosh Hashanah to symbolize a sweet life?"

"That's just a coincidence."

"Let's look them up in the Bible."

"You really believe the two *altekockers* were direct descendants of Abraham and Sarah?" Papa chuckled and wrapped Anya in a bear cub hug.

"Speaking of old and wise, look who's up in the middle of the night. Chaim, to what do we owe this pleasure? You haven't joined me for midnight prayers since your last gall bladder attack."

Dedushka limped toward them, holding a pair of shiny shoes. "Take them." He placed the new but old-fashioned shoes in Papa's hands. "To protect you in Nanjing. My *zayde* gave me these powerful shoes for my annual pilgrimage to the *tzaddik*."

"Did Vulcan make these shoes?" Anya knew how to get Dedushka's goat.

"Stop filling your head with the antics of those ridiculous Greeks."

"Vulcan made golden shoes that gave the wearer the ability to travel at the speed of wind *and* walk on water."

"I can guarantee you Vulcan wasn't as powerful as my *tzaddik*, a man who was a great blessing to the men who sat at his feet. I carried these shoes in my knapsack. I walked barefoot for weeks, across dry fields and dirt roads, never alone. God was with me and my comrades—the fathers, sons, and nephews from the villages I passed who joined the trek. Only forty times did I wear these shoes. Only once a year did the soles touch the backs of my thighs—never the floor—as I knelt in front of Reb Zalman, the Tzaddik.

"Joshua, these shoes will bring you luck and wisdom. Wear them and you won't need to ask Athena for advice."

"Dedushka!" Anya put her hands on her hips. "You, too? Don't tell me Mama read you the myths at the same time as Papa."

"What do you mean 'Mama read'?" Dedushka said. "*I* read. When your Mama was a little girl, I read *her* the myths."

Once Papa and Dedushka went back into their bedrooms, Anya crept downstairs to the kitchen. She wasn't a bit tired. When Anya was a baby, Papa had called her a jumping bean; now that she was a teenager, he used a more grown-up word: insomniac. She poured the remaining half cup of soy milk from the pail into a saucepan. When the first bubbles rose to the surface and popped, she turned off the flame and took a sip. Warm soy milk was sweeter and creamier than milk. Good, this would help her relax and sleep.

A moth fluttered near the lightbulb. *Stupid moth. Thus hath the candle sing'd the moth.* Even Shakespeare knew that moths weren't intelligent enough to avoid getting burned. She could catch it and take it outside but Li Mei had warned her to leave moths alone, especially the ones that flew into the kitchen when the Hungry Ghost Moon was full. "If you see a moth acting like a ghost, call it good brother or you will anger the gods. And when the moon is Hungry Ghost, be home before dark. And don't wander the streets at night. And stay out of the swimming pool at the recreation grounds. Spirits like to drown people."

The Chinese manuals have more rules than the Talmud.

Anya cupped her hands and tried repeatedly to catch the moth. On the fourth attempt she succeeded but the tip of her thumb grazed the hot glass.

"Ouch!"

"What's wrong, Anya? Do you need help?" *How long has Gabriel been watching me from the kitchen door?* He rushed over to help her. His eyes were spilling with concern.

"I was trying not to hurt the moth and I burned my finger. I need to set it free in the garden."

They stared at each other for a minute. Anya should have been nervous about a boy seeing her dressed in a nightgown and robe. But she wasn't. She felt natural, as though they had known each other always.

Gabriel followed her outdoors. "It's so quiet. Where's the typhoon? Or was that weather report just a stunt to trap Papi and me for the night?"

"I'm sure Georgi called the BBC commentator and arranged the announcement for exactly that reason." Anya laughed. "But if you ask Dedushka, he'll tell you the midnight prayers sent the storm back across the Yellow Sea!"

Gabriel was amused by Anya's jokes. She could tell by his wink that he appreciated her humor.

She pointed to the sky. "See that moon? It's called *dashu*."

"I thought it was the Hungry Ghost Moon."

"Shhhh! Don't talk so loud. A ghost might hear you and hunt us down."

"You, and Li Mei, are *not* scaring me. But Li Mei tried, all right. She pulled me aside after the card game and warned me not to swim until August."

"Li Mei knows everything, so you better listen," Anya said. "Aren't you curious about what *dashu* means?"

"I bet you'll tell me anyway."

"*Dashu* means 'great heat.' My first week in China, the moon was *ta han*. 'Great cold.' See! We are opposites!"

A cry, louder than their flirtatious laughter, caught their attention.

"I know that sound!" Anya said. "Kisa is awake."

"You have a baby sister?"

"Not yet. But Mama is pregnant. The crying baby is Kisa, a foundling. I brought her home this afternoon from the alley."

"You are not kidding me, Bella Anya?"

"No. It is true. I'll show you."

Anya and Gabriel peered down the dark staircase to the servants' quarters. Kisa's cries seemed to echo off the walls. They couldn't see past the first step and carefully felt around with their soles before stepping full weight. Each step creaked like a ghost's old bones. Anya shivered, tempted to run back up the steps to the safety of the warm kitchen. Gabriel grabbed her hand.

A light glowed from the doorway of the room at the bottom of the stairs. Anya pulled Gabriel with her into the laundry room. Dandan was feeding the sleeve of one of Papa's white dress shirts into the wringer of the washer. Papa's cuff didn't get caught or wrap around itself, like the time Anya tried to operate the new machine, but rolled easily through to the tub of rinse water. Mo-chou hummed as she ironed the last crease of Papa's underpants.

"Miss Ani-ah, it is late! Does your mah-mee know you are sneaking around at all hours with the boy from Italy?"

Gabriel's eyes widened and he seemed antsy but Anya was unfazed by Dandan's question. "It's fine, Gabriel. Once Mama puts in her ear plugs, she's dead to the world."

"I don't plan on getting in trouble with a girl from Odessa! Maybe we should go back to our rooms."

"Careful with my bowling uniform, please. I won't throw a strike if the collar is starched stiff." Anya made a mental note to remember, for once, to bring Mo-chou a moon cake after Tuesday's practice. The top and shorts were always crisp thanks to her handiwork with the new electric iron.

"Do you two always work this late?" Gabriel asked.

"This is early, Master Gabe. We don't finish our chores until two a.m. Madame expects the house to run smoothly and we must please her."

"Better you than me," Anya joked. "I mean the part about two a.m."

"Make that baby stop crying like a goat," Dandan said to Anya.

"Anya, let's go. I want to meet your orphan baby," Gabriel said.

Back in the hall, the shadows played tricks with Anya's imagination and she was glad Gabriel had come with her downstairs. He squeezed her fingers, and they sprinted through the cement passageway toward the line of light on the ground at the end of the hall. Anya slid open the pocket door to Li Mei and Dandan's shared room.

Li Mei looked over her shoulder at Anya and Gabriel, but didn't stop braiding her hair. She coiled the shiny ponytail around the crown of her head. *How does she braid so perfectly without a mirror? If only my hair were as silky, every strand in place.* Anya thought Li Mei's neck was more graceful than a swan's. Kisa was lying in a birch basket at Li Mei's feet, kicking her legs above her belly, and gurgling.

Gabriel walked directly to the basket and knelt down. "Do you think she knows she's lost?" he asked.

"Not like Amelia Earhart knows she's lost," Anya said. *If no one can find you, but you are somewhere, are you truly lost?*

"If Amelia Earhart is still alive, I bet she misses her mother." Gabriel turned his face away. A muscle in his jaw quivered. Anya imagined him lying facedown on his pillow, damp with tears of loneliness for home.

"Everybody, even grown-ups, miss their mothers. I miss Jia Li every night. When her face pops into my mind, I smell ginger, and I know I am precious to someone. Someday, I will live with her again."

I can't imagine missing this strange Shanghai mama. But I do wish Mama B.C. would come back.

Li Mei sang the first lines of a lullaby. Although Anya didn't know the lyrics, she hummed the soothing melody. Candlelight flickered on Gabriel's and Kisa's faces.

Li Mei stooped and picked up Kisa. "Sit, if you want to hold her," she said to Gabriel, and gestured at the tufted stool.

"Me?" Gabriel asked.

"Yes, you!" Anya giggled.

Gabriel's face blanched, then reddened, but he sat down and held out his arms. Li Mei lay Kisa in Gabriel's lap and showed him how to position his hands to secure her from falling.

"Isn't she too young for jewelry?" Gabriel asked. He wiggled the tiny padlock strung on the silver necklace around the baby's neck.

"This chain links her to life," Li Mei said, "according to Chinese custom."

"Why can't we keep her?" Anya said. She raised her eyebrows, knowing the answer but asking anyway. "At least until the little indentation in her head fills out or her belly button falls off? The Talmud says it's a mitzvah to bring up an orphan as though she were one's daughter—or sister."

"You are a very smart girl but you may not decide these things," Li Mei said. "She is not an orphan."

"You don't know that. Her mother might have jumped in the river," Anya said.

"I am most certain Kisa's mother is alive. Jules called here a few hours ago to make sure we knew the storm was upgraded to a typhoon. When I said I would be traveling to Siccawei with the newborn girl Miss Ani-ah found, he wanted to know every detail because a haggard gentry woman, who recently gave birth, collapsed in the rectory before dinner. When Father Matteo revived her, she mumbled in formal Mandarin that she had broken her sacred promise to provide her husband with a male heir. Fearing for her baby girl's life, she ran away with her daughter before her father-in-law heard the news. She has been hiding in the gardens of a villa in Frenchtown, stealing food from refugees for the past two days."

"How do you know she's Kisa's mother? Was she wearing a yellow dress?" Anya blurted.

"She claims she left her baby in a basket, and waited in the shadows until a girl on a red bicycle discovered her daughter. The girl chased her across the Bridge of Nine Turns, didn't catch her because she had bribed the proprietress of Huxinting Tea House to hide her in the latrine."

"That woman must have a heart of stone," Gabriel said. His eyes were sad.

"She is *not* cruel, Gabriel," said Li Mei. "Many mothers in the same situation would drown their babies. If she hadn't stolen away with Kisa, her husband would have disposed of his useless baby girl."

"No baby is useless! How do you know the mother is telling the truth?" Gabriel retorted.

"Once I was old enough to milk the goats, I helped Jia Li cook for the orphans at Tushanwan. We also fed runaway mothers. I listened to many stories, many truths. Girls are not allowed to worship at the Ancestral Tablet or carry on the family name. If a man decides an evil spirit has possessed a baby, it is decided. If a pig died on the day she was born, the farmer blames her. If a tiny tooth sticks out from her gums, the elders say, 'This girl will eat the family's profits.'"

"Is Kisa's mother still at Siccawei?" Anya asked. "Can I meet her? Can we leave now?"

"*You* aren't going anywhere. I will take her tomorrow as I promised your papa and mama. After I feed your family Shabbat breakfast."

"But what about her checkup with Dr. Miller?" Anya said.

"The Jesuit doctor at Siccawei will give her a thorough examination, including her billy rubies."

"It's 'bilirubin,' Li Mei! I looked it up. The bilirubin level in the baby's urine measures liver function," Anya said.

"You sound like a *doctore*," Gabriel said.

"Please let me go with you, Li Mei. No one needs to know. We can leave after I walk Amelia and Pidge at French Park."

"How do you walk canaries?" Gabriel asked.

Anya ignored him and dropped to her knees. "I deserve to meet Kisa's mother. I saved her baby."

"It is too risky, Miss Ani-ah." Li Mei took Kisa from Gabriel, laid her over her shoulder gently, and caressed the baby's back in an upward motion. Kisa burped twice. "Ai-yah. You have some nerve, Miss Ani-ah. I almost lost my job tonight."

"At least tell me the mother's name."

"Jules said she refuses to reveal her family name or where her husband's estate is located." Li Mei bent over and nuzzled Kisa's ear. "Don't worry, baby. We'll keep you safe."

Anya asked, "When *will* you take me there?" She tried not to sound harsh, as if she was ordering a mere servant to do her bidding.

"When your parents aren't watching," Li Mei said sharply, and narrowed her sleepy eyes. She spread her bare feet wide and jutted her chin.

And that is that! Anya realized. *I better stop asking or Li Mei will embarrass me in front of Gabriel.*

Li Mei continued, "We'll take the trolley. Maybe next week. I told Jules I would help Jia Li teach the woman how to cook. The Jesuits will provide food and shelter for her and the baby but will require her to work in exchange for their keep."

"Like a commoner?"

"If I didn't know better, I'd call you a spoiled rich girl! There is nothing common about kindness! Or the food I prepare for your family."

Oh my God. Will I ever learn when to speak up and when to keep my mouth shut? "I'm sorry, Li Mei. I didn't mean to insult you," Anya said, and though she tried not to, began to weep.

Gabriel put his arm around Anya's shoulder. He didn't say a word. He didn't try to talk her out of crying. He let her be.

Li Mei, on the other hand, told Anya to shush and reminded her, "When eating bamboo sprouts, you must remember the woman who planted them." She knelt down and pushed aside the straw mat next to her bed. She lifted a plank and, from the hole, pulled out a pouch. "I've saved every *yuan* your papa has paid me to donate to Tushanwan one day. *If* I can persuade Mah-mee to let me return."

Anya cried, "Please stay with us until I leave for America. You are one of my only friends in Shanghai, besides Giselle."

"Hey?" Gabriel said. "What about me?"

Li Mei blinked back tears, dropped the pouch in the secret compartment, and covered the floorboards. After she straightened the throw rug, she bowed to Anya and Gabriel. "Go to your rooms, you two."

Anya shook Kisa's tiny hand and said, "*Do svidanya,* until we meet again."

"*Ciao,*" Gabriel said, and kissed first one, then the other of Li Mei's cheeks.

They left the room, climbed up the servants' stairs, then the stairway to the second-floor bedrooms. The skylight in the stairwell ceiling framed the moon with a starry backdrop.

The moon is shining even brighter than my birthday moon last night. Maybe the wind cleaned the air.

"The last moon I saw in Odessa winked at me," Anya said.

"Or maybe the wink was a cloud floating by the spot where an eye would be if the moon was a face," Gabriel said. His tone was soft, not the attitude of a know-it-all.

"When I miss Odessa, I pretend the Odessa moon watched me get on the train and then the ship, and followed me to Shanghai."

"The moon is the same in Italy as Odessa and Shanghai," Gabriel replied.

He squeezed her hand and stopped in front of Anya's bedroom door.

Is he going to kiss me twice, too? Are his lips soft? Will I like the feeling of Gabriel's mouth pressed against mine?

As Big Ching and the cuckoo clock on the hope chest chimed once, Gabriel leaned his face into Anya's. "*Ciao, bella,*" he whispered, then planted a gentle kiss on her forehead and turned toward Georgi's door.

Anya floated into her bedroom. Her first kiss and a smile were warm on her face.

fourteen

efore Big Ching had finished its seventh chime, Pidge's urgent chirp awakened Anya. She sprang from her bed and pulled on her seersucker shorts and cotton blouse. She had fidgeted like popping corn most of the night, thinking about how different Gabriel was from Bobby. But she didn't feel tired. She secured her hair with a pair of ivory chopsticks, checked the bun in the mirror, then went out on the terrace barefoot.

She watched Li Mei harvesting heads of purple cabbage in the garden below. Dandan plucked a handful of beans and dropped them in a basket. They moved next to neat rows of beet and carrot tops. Li Mei began to chant, "Pearly dew of the jade heavens, golden waves of Buddha's ocean, may a drop become a flood and purify mountains and rivers."

Her rain dance is next, Anya predicted. Sure enough, Li Mei rocked her head from side to side, and shook her hips. She looked up at Anya and called out, "Stingy *dah fong* provided one measly bucket of rain last night. My carrots sipped one drop, my beets the other, before the typhoon blew away and disappeared over Little Kunshan Mountain."

"Good! I hope all the beets in China rot," Anya said. She wished Li Mei didn't serve beet soup in the summer but Babushka insisted on borscht with lunch. Even Li Mei admitted she hated beets because the juice stained her fingers. The only good thing about the soup was searching for the bay leaf in the bowl. Whoever found it would get mail that day.

"Any chance you changed your mind about Siccawei?" Anya called.

"*Nyet*, as your papa would say!"

Anya plastered her poor-me-pity-me expression on her face but there was no point in trying to stare Li Mei down. Li Mei never changed her mind once she'd said no in Russian.

Anya ran back into her room, fastened the clasps on her sandals, and put Amelia and Pidge in their little walking cages. She jogged down the stairs as fast as she could without bumping into the walls.

The samovar was lit and surrounded by eight *potstikanis*, eight silver spoons, a bowl of sugar cubes, and sliced lemon for Anya. She retrieved a slice of leftover challah, and planted kisses on Papa's, then Mama's cheeks as they poured their tea.

"Good morning, Anya. Hot enough for you today?" Papa said, and pretended to tip a hat at her. He set his *potstikani* at the head of the table and tore off his khaki coat, then unbuttoned the top button of his collar and loosened his belt.

Why does he bother dressing in his suit on Shabbat when he ends up partially undressed before breakfast is over?

"The temperature will be ninety-seven degrees by two and stay in the nineties into this evening," Papa said. Between bites of his cold borscht and cucumber salad, he picked dill from his teeth.

Mama said, "I'm going to *shvitz*."

"Take off your stockings, Stellachka. That's why you're sweating like a—" Papa said.

"Mama perspires. She doesn't sweat!" Anya pointed out.

"And I'd think twice about calling a pregnant woman a pig, if I were you," Mama added.

I won't ever wear stockings, Anya thought as she gulped her tea. She fished the lemon slice from the bottom of the cup when Mama wasn't watching, peeled the thin rind from around the fruit, and popped it on her tongue. Anya was the only member of the family who could eat a lemon without puckering.

"I'll set up a fan for you in your room," Papa offered to Mama.

Mr. Benatar and Gabriel sauntered into the dinette area. They were dressed in the same clothes as last night. Papa pushed back his chair and shook their hands, and tousled Gabriel's hair. "How did you sleep?"

"*Tranquillo,*" Mr. Benatar said. "But Gabriel was another story. He tossed and turned all night. I don't know what's gotten into him." He winked at Anya.

Blush number twenty-three in less than twenty-four hours was a record for Anya. She looked down at her napkin so no one, especially not Gabriel, would see her burning cheeks.

"Sit." Papa pointed at the two chairs on the garden side of

the table. "Enjoy a bowl of my mamele's famous *cholent*. It simmered in the stew pot, untouched—not a single stir—for twelve hours."

"Your father tells us you celebrated your fourteenth birthday on Thursday. You and my Gabriel are the same age," Mr. Benatar said.

"Actually, she is older than I by three months and four days," Gabriel said. "Did you make an offering to your Juno on your birthday?" he asked Anya.

Papa's consternation spread over his face like a grimace. "Only pagans make offerings to *many* gods. Jews worship *one* God."

"He is joking, of course," Mr. Benatar said. "In the Roman birthday custom, boys give gifts to their Geniuses, or protective spirits, girls to their Junos."

"Papi, I can speak for myself," Gabriel said.

"*I* know who Juno was," Georgi piped in. "She decorated her pet peacock's tail with Argus's one hundred eyes after Mercury cut his head off. I bet you didn't know *that* about peacock feathers!" Georgi crossed his arms over his chest, looking extremely proud of himself.

"Speaking of feathers," Mama said, "remove those dirty cages to the garden while we eat, Anush. I don't want birdseeds sprinkled on my eggs!"

"No, don't!" Georgi said. "What if a hungry alley cat is waiting to pounce?"

Mama flashed her that-is-that look and he shoved another spoonful of beef stew in his mouth.

As Anya picked the cages up, Gabriel jumped up to help

her. She handed him Pidge, and their fingers brushed. A feeling of heat, not from the weather, rushed up her arm to her chest. Her heart pounded. She sensed Gabriel was trying not to smile but the corners of his mouth gave him away.

By the time Anya and Gabriel sat back down at the table, Anya couldn't remember where they stashed the cages or if they had spoken to one another. *What is happening to me?*

Papa had changed the subject to politics. "Your King Victor Emmanuel is a coward!"

Anya expected Mr. Benatar to take offence. *For once could Papa skip the controversial topics,* Anya pleaded silently. *Even his warnings about the ten most dangerous fruits to avoid in summer would be better than hearing another word about Hitler and Mussolini.*

"I agree wholeheartedly, Joshua. If our king doesn't pay attention, that Fascist megalomaniac Mussolini will overrun Italy."

"At least our trains are running on time now," Gabriel said, and looked at his father. They fell into a fit of laughter.

So much happiness in the Benatar family! We used to enjoy our conversations, too.

"What a coincidence, Gabriel, that our new friends live on a street across the world named after our occasionally esteemed king."

That was the kind of coincidence that usually possessed Dedushka to ramble on and on about the mystics and numerology. But he was quiet, then in a slow rumble said, "If your King Victor forms an alliance with Hitler, the Jews will suffer. We have been scapegoats since the beginning of time. I've lived through three pogroms. If Hitler gains more power in Europe, there will be no stopping angry crowds with torches and hatchets killing innocent Jews for no reason except that they are Jewish. Hitler is worse than Stalin and the czars combined."

"An unbearable situation in Europe. Thanks God we are free in China," Papa said, and bowed his head.

When Papa said "thanks" in plural, that meant double the appreciation. In contrast to the warning about the fate of the Jews, it sounded as if a curse had struck Italy, Germany, and Poland.

Anya swallowed the last bite of leftover strudel and asked if she may be excused to walk her birds. No one answered her— the adults were engaged in talk of the Nazis marching through Eastern Europe.

She gestured for Gabriel to follow her. "Last night you asked how I walk my birds. Want to see? Giselle will meet us on the corner. If her parents let her out of the house this morning."

Gabriel accepted her invitation by scooting his chair back from the table and following her outside. Anya handed him Pidge's cage. He held it at arm's length, then peered in.

"I've never walked a cage before!"

They made their way in silence down the driveway, along the stone wall covered with glossy leaves and star jasmine blossoms. A pair of turtledoves alighted on the iron bars of the trellis. The rose garden seemed to be in full bloom, despite the lack of rain.

"Don't pick any flowers. You never know which one is a goddess in disguise." Anya turned to face him.

"Are you suggesting this bush is Lotis the nymph hiding from a lovesick pursuer?"

He passed my test. He has read the myths, Anya thought, and smiled to herself.

"In Italy, our teachers read the myths aloud every year beginning with kindergarten. We memorized the Roman version, not the Greeks'."

"Okay, show-off, why was Dryope punished?"

"That's easy! Because she didn't know Lotis was in disguise as the purple flower she had just picked until blood began to drip from the stems." Gabriel pushed out his chin in mock indignation.

"And her punishment was . . . ?"

He put down the cage and swung both arms into a U shape above his head to look like the crown of a tree, his arm muscles pulling his sleeves tight. He swayed his branches with his thighs held together straight as a tree trunk.

"Good answer. But what *kind* of tree did she turn into?" Anya said, annoyed that her face was flushing again at the sight of Gabriel's strong body.

"A lotus, perhaps?" Gabriel teased.

Anya opened the front gate and pivoted on her right foot and spun to step out backward. She stopped herself. She didn't want Gabriel to think she was superstitious. She made a half turn, then walked through the gate.

I want to face forward to see where I'm going!

On the corner, they waited for a couple of minutes for Giselle. Gabriel tapped his foot on the sidewalk, and said, "I bet your best friend doesn't actually exist!" He elbowed her lightly in the ribs in jest.

"Her mother must have sprung a recital on the family. Mr. Lindberg sticks to the Shabbat laws on Friday nights but not on Saturdays if it involves Giselle's little brother, Archie, and his precious violin."

"Let's go!" Anya led Gabriel through the *lilong*, rushing so they wouldn't be late. "*Vite!*"

When they arrived at the hedged entrance of French Park, Gabriel pointed at the rainbow arching over the temple in the distance. Anya chanted the blessing upon seeing pleasing sights. *He notices little things like I do*, she thought, pleased that this enchanting boy came into her life when she didn't expect him.

Gabriel nodded in cadence with the beat of the drums and stared at the flurry of cylindrical, hexagonal, multilevel, and partitioned birdcages on parade. Anya sidled into her usual spot behind Madame Baubigny and her myna bird named Antoinette. She made room for Gabriel in line next to her.

"*Bonjour*, Madame," Anya said.

"*Bonjour*, Madame," mimicked Antoinette, whose imitation of Anya's French was pitch-perfect. Anya had worked diligently with her French tutor to master an authentic accent.

Gabriel howled with laughter and each time Antoinette parroted Anya's introductions to her fellow bird walkers, Anya and he giggled louder. She watched Gabriel's eyes dart from one sight to another, reminding her of how curious *she* was six months ago, the day she rode with her family in a caravan of rickshaws from the jetty to their new house.

She wondered what Gabriel missed about Italy. Did he, too,

remember little details about his old house? *My curtain flutter-ing out the gap between the window sash and sill. The bump on the stepping-stone I used to trip over on the path to our back door. Valentina's cooking rules, such as, "One second before sweet cream butter turns brown, you will hear a sizzle in the pan, if you listen closely."*

Was it harder waiting in the January cold on a "four-coat winter day" or dripping with sweat in the dust of July, gunfire blasting on the other side of Soochow Creek, and hungry ghosts haunting every corner?

"Do you miss your friends?" Anya asked him.

"Papi and I are only in Shanghai for a year. Before long, I'll see Sam and Tony again."

"You didn't answer my question," Anya said, and immediately wished she could take back her mild accusation. She worried she had been too forward.

Gabriel didn't appear to be fazed. They looped three more times around the park lawn and headed for the exit gate. That's when Anya spied Li Mei, carrying Kisa in a sling, waiting at the corner of Boulevard de Deux Républiques for the trolley.

"Aren't you dying to know more about Kisa's mother?" Anya asked Gabriel.

"You bet I am. Will you ring me after Li Mei gets back this afternoon and tell me what she found out?"

"I have a better idea! How about my firsthand impression? I'll take photos, too."

"Anya." The way he said her name as a warning sounded much like Papa's voice.

147

"Gabriel, please help me! Li Mei is about to get on the trolley. I can sneak on the back. But I need you to take Amelia and Pidge back to my room. Okay?"

Anya thrust Amelia's cage into his other hand and didn't wait for an answer. She dashed toward the trolley, and blew Gabriel a kiss as she climbed the steps.

fifteen

Anya pushed to the middle of the car where Li Mei was
seated, narrowly missing a spray of spit from a boy getting off the vehicle. The trolley lurched as it gained speed and
Anya practically fell into Li Mei's lap.

"Ai-yah!" Li Mei said. "I had a feeling from the minute I left
the house that I would run into you. I even planned what I
would say to your papa if he found out you disobeyed."

"What?"

"Never mind, for Kwan Yin's sake!" Li Mei nudged Anya
with her foot. "See the mother and baby near the doors. He's
wearing the trousers I told you about, with a hole in the bottom
and a flap with a snap sewn over it."

"Will Kisa's mother actually cut a hole in her baby's bloomers?"

"No bother, no mess. Instead of changing diapers all day,
many mothers find an outhouse, unsnap the flap, and hold their
child over the toilet bowl."

"That's absurd. We have real diapers in Odessa."

"You're in Shanghai. Remember?"

Li Mei adjusted Kisa's sling. She looked closely at the baby's face and frowned. "I am worried for her. A newborn is supposed to stay at her mother's breast in a dark room for a month before she sees the sun."

The trolley passed White Cloud Monastery. Anya followed the outline of the spire that rose higher than the other roof lines in the Old City. She counted the seven stories of the octagonal tower and called out, "Gold, silver, pottery glaze, pearl, agate, rose, and giant clam," punctuating the last item with a nod of her chin.

"See, Li Mei! I memorized your lesson about the treasures."

"Why does anyone care about stupid old clams?" A boy's voice shouted from behind their seat. "They taste nasty."

"Georgi?" Anya turned and glared at her brother. "What the heck are you doing on this trolley? Go home!"

Li Mei's mouth tightened. "Did you dream up another way to get me fired, since it didn't work last night?" She turned around and pulled his ear until he stood up. "Your mother will have a fit if she finds out that not one but both of her children are on a trolley on Shabbat!"

"Georgi, go back the way you came," Anya pleaded.

"I don't know the way, Annie. I followed Li Mei here."

He lost his balance as the trolley started rolling.

"At the next stop, the two of you get off and go straight home!" Li Mei ordered. "No arguments."

"Unfair!" Anya glared at Li Mei and jerked Georgi's hand. "Georgi, you're going to pay!"

"I will tell Kisa's mother the story of how you brought her baby home," Li Mei said.

Anya dragged Georgi through the back door. She was so mad she didn't remember to wave good-bye to Kisa until the car had whirred away. She strode several paces ahead of her brother and yelled over her shoulder, "You better move it, or I'll turn a corner and you'll be stuck on this scary boulevard by yourself and an army truck will hit you."

Georgi trotted so fast to keep up with Anya that he almost bumped into a red-turbaned Sikh directing traffic from a position surrounded by sandbags. His bushy black beard was oiled and the ends of his mustache were twisted up like a smile, and coiled like snakes around his chin. He blasted his whistle at Georgi.

"Anya, I'm dying of hunger for soup. Hot soup."

"On a blistering day like this? You're not eating soup," Anya said.

"You don't eat it, dummy, you drink it."

Had Anya not been furious with her brother, and had it not been forbidden to handle money on Shabbat, she might have bought him an icy slice of watermelon or a ginger ice cream cone with the penny she had tucked in the pocket of her camera bag. But she calmed down by the time they passed the fourth soup seller on Avenue Joffre.

I've already broken so many rules. What does one more matter?

The fifth seller used a glass pyramid over the stock pot to protect the broth from horseflies and pigeon droppings. He wiped the inside of a willow-patterned bowl with a rag, and assembled the soup from seven saucers on his cart, then filled the bowl with boiling water and squirted a few dashes of soy sauce on top. Anya prayed that the ingredients, which resembled dirty sugar, insect eggs, and chartreuse-colored lichen, were edible and wouldn't give Georgi gas.

Georgi smacked his lips and sniffed the bowl in mock ecstasy. Anya fished for her coins and slowly counted, making sure the seller saw her worried look. She zipped the pocket and turned to walk away.

That's good for a price reduction. She held out another few seconds and he offered an even lower price.

The closest empty stoop was at least seven body lengths from where they stood. Anya carried the bowl for Georgi so not a drop would be wasted in a spill.

"Stay close to me."

"Give me the soup already! Do you want me to pass out?"

"Once you are sitting, you can have the bowl back."

They traversed the line of refugees waiting for free bowls of rice from the distribution center. A little boy banging with an iron stick on a bamboo tube–drum knocked Anya's elbow, causing a wave of soup to swish over the lip of the bowl and sizzle on the pavement.

Georgi sat Indian-style on the landing and, once settled, reached for the soup like a beggar. *He acts like a glutton.* He slurped, and crunched hungrily on the mystery chunks that had sunk to the bottom of the bowl.

Little boys and girls wove in and out of the streams of strolling parents and amahs, running, screaming, pushing, giggling, fencing, some even trying to jump rope and juggle oranges, despite the crowd of refugees pushing wheelbarrows piled with bedding, clothing, and pots without lids. A boy no older than three tailed his father carrying a small cardboard sign which read

BOY FOR SALE. He would fetch a good price from someone who needed an adopted son to work hard and carry on the family name. Girls were a different story. They were bought as *mooitsai* for a small sum. These slaves had the potential of becoming future daughters-in-law if they bore sons. Only then would the clans release the girls from slave duties.

When Georgi finished, Anya walked back to the seller to return the bowl. *How unjust to sell children. I guess it's better than drowning them.* She didn't see the pile of black and yellow watermelon seeds dotting the pavement like a swarm of bees. She slipped, and before she fell to the ground was sandwiched between a rickshaw puller and a trio of large men, and swept away from where Georgi waited for her to return.

"Georgi," she gasped. "Over here . . . on the double."

He was jumping up and down. He didn't lock eyes with her but on the fourth or fifth jump apparently spotted her over the tops of heads.

"Wait for me, Annie!" he shouted, then disappeared into the crowd.

What if I lose Georgi? An awful thing could happen to him. She ducked from one tight clog of people to the next. The flood swept her into the entryway of Great World Amusement Palace, Georgi's favorite forbidden place in Shanghai. A few months ago, Li Mei snuck them in here on an evening when Mama was in rehearsals at the Lyceum and Papa had sailed to Tsingtao to report on the U.S. Navy maneuvers. She had threatened to hire a local ear wax extractor to dig in their ear canals if they mentioned one word about the outing to either of their parents.

Anya flattened herself against the wall so the throng wouldn't pull her up the ramp. *Where is my little brother?* She screamed his name. She pulled at her hair. No one would let her cross to the other side of the foyer. She pinched the back of a woman's arm hoping she'd stop to rub the sore spot, giving Anya room to lunge through the whip of people.

Finally, she found Georgi in the aisle of the main theater. She grabbed him and hugged him and whispered, *Thanks God!* She was still a little mad at him, but her relief wiped out her earlier frustration.

"Papa doesn't have to know we're here. Can we go upstairs?" Georgi asked. "We'll explain it wasn't our fault that we were pushed inside."

What is wrong with letting him have a little fun?

"But I'll be punished, not you."

"No one has to find out."

"You can't keep a secret."

"I swear I will."

Anya held out her pinkie. "Swear on my life? No, make that Mama's."

He wrapped his pinkie around hers. "Swear."

He plopped in an empty seat in the first row. Loud and sudden as a train's approach, a mix of voices yelled at him, "Get up! Those seats are reserved for the spirits! It is bad form to sit there."

They ran from the room and up the ramp to the second floor. Anya batted away the delving hand of a pickpocket. One more turn and they arrived at the third-floor fun house. At the entrance, a roving magician pulled an apple-green jade medallion from behind Anya's ear lobe and said, "Real cheap, this jade is yours. Only twenty coppers." She shook her head and put her hand up to push him away.

She found Georgi across the hallway watching live turtles fly high into the air. The juggler said, "I've been waiting for you, boy, to come along and feed my rock turtles. You are very lucky I chose you, little man. This will increase your merit."

Georgi giggled and looked at Anya for permission.

"What are you waiting for? *Chop-chop*," the juggler said. "These turtles are very busy being lazy today. They're as hungry as alligators."

He shoved a hard cake in Georgi's hand and Georgi dropped it into the carp-filled tank. A school of gigantic striped fish wrestled one another under a miniature bridge. Perched above them, the family of rock turtles didn't budge, even after Georgi prodded them with his finger.

"Let's get out of here," Anya said. "That man is scheming for us to buy a pet turtle."

They pushed through a clump of illiterates waiting in line while the letter writer composed love notes, letters, marriage contracts—whatever documents they needed for ten *yuan* per page, extra for calligraphy. One man cut the line and the rest of the crowd gave him a tongue-lashing. So many arguments, spitting, people staring.

Next, they ran through the mirror maze. Georgi beat Anya to the exit only because she stopped to examine her face to check if her pimple had returned. Near the tall, fire-red doors, they were caught in another twist of people and Georgi disappeared again.

A midwife offered to deliver babies. Firecrackers popped. A

blue balloon floated above Anya's head. The stuffy heat made her dizzy.

There's the love letter booth. Giselle says it guarantees results. She could win a boy's affections with the help of a romantic professional. But once she saw the love expert's fee, she figured she could call on Cupid himself to fly over from Mount Olympus, find Gabriel, and shoot the barbed points of two magic arrows into his heart.

Come to think of it, Cupid has already done his job! I don't care anymore about going to Bobby Sassoon's bowling party.

A display of bamboo cages buzzed with cricket song. There were miniature round cages and cubes with sliding doors. Her favorite was a sandalwood cage with ivory mosaic corners.

"You want to save money. Buy this one with no doors. The katydid is woven in," the seller said. "You want a small cricket? How about Huang Ling, my little golden bell? Or Mo Ling, an inky bell?"

He rattled off six more choices. Anya's head swam with the names. She shook her head at each option. She didn't want to rush her decision.

A singsong girl, wearing a tattered blue gown, limped over on one shoe and watched awhile, fanning herself. "What's wrong, white girl?" Her lips were blood red with lipstick drawn outside the pouty edges.

To the seller, she said, "Big boy, give the girl what she wants. Stop haggling."

"Boys like these fighting crickets to kill the Japs."

Anya frowned. She looked once more at each cage and found the perfect one near the end of the bottom row labeled

JIAO GE-GE. She pointed to it and asked, "What does that word mean in English?"

The singsong girl said, "*Jiao Ge-Ge* means 'Singing Brother.'"

"I will put him in a pot for better sound. Only a little more money." The seller pointed to a selection of brick-red clay pots embellished with carvings of dragons, phoenix, bats, or lotus—symbols of good luck.

"I want a tube to keep the cricket in my pocket."

"Real cheap I'll sell you this bamboo and reed tube. Fancy breathing cover and feeder at the bottom. Okie-dokie?"

Anya paid without haggling and slid the cricket into its new house. She bet she'd find Georgi on the sixth-floor seesaw. And she did. She watched him jump on one end. It sank to the ground with a thud. The boy on the other end was much lighter and flew through the air each time Georgi pumped his pudgy legs.

Mosquitoes buzzed from one of Anya's ears to the other, so loudly it sounded like bees and mosquitoes, *and* flies. She batted at the air. *I don't need a slew of red bites on my face that will swell and cause Babushka to start calling me Pimpleface again.*

More and more mosquitoes roared in her ears. Anya realized the buzzing wasn't the sound of insects. The noise frightened her.

Georgi jumped off the seesaw and pointed up at the cloud cover. He threw his cap into the air and clapped at the sight of a plane's underbelly. One of the planes dipped its nose as though nodding hello. When Anya read about the Hindenburg dirigible falling from the sky in New Jersey a few weeks ago, she couldn't understand why the spectators hadn't run before it exploded.

Now she did. She froze with fear. *Planes here?* Something was awfully wrong.

Georgi yelled, "Look, Anya! Curtiss Hawks from the Chinese Eighty-seventh division! And Northrops!"

Hoots and whistles greeted the low-flying planes. A Dalmatian opened and closed its mouth, without making the barking sound, showed its teeth, and whipped its tail between its hind legs. That's when Anya realized how loud the engines were. The dog mime-barked in slow motion as its owner scratched its rump. What she could hear was her heart hammering faster than a baby's. The sound of it beating in her ears unnerved her. She pushed her fingers into her ear canals but the sensation and noise worsened.

She seized Georgi's arm and dragged him toward the ramp.

Closer and closer, the whizzing sound came. Her arms and legs moved without intention, nowhere to go. If only she could disappear with Georgi into a thick cloud the way Diana the huntress magically escaped from pursuers. *I am on my own, no one to rely on but myself. My imagination is not going to save us. Closer and closer. Wu wei, go with the river. I am waiting to die. I am waiting to stay alive.*

Anya had an urge to jump into the arms of the woman with wide eyes. The edge of the seesaw bounced on the pavement. Georgi hid his face in the folds of her blouse.

I'm not ready. Don't let Mama find our bodies. If only she hadn't sent Gabriel on ahead.

Anya held Georgi tight. *This is what happens when you don't obey.*

The bomb hit. Anya smelled smoke, tasted the gusts of

wind. A gasp licked the ramp like flames. *A bomb? From Chinese planes?* Anya staggered and covered her head, bursting from the pressure in her ears. She sprinted, pulling Georgi with her, around the first curve, the next, and the next. They neared the red doors and slowed.

The doors were closed. Georgi coughed and coughed. People pushed against their backs. Anya couldn't breathe. If she hadn't listened to Papa's warnings to close her ears whenever Li Mei told a *farkakte* tale, she could now use Li Mei's magic to transform the line of people into a river strong enough to burst open the doors. Li Mei's stories weren't nonsense! Not if the Taoist magic could float her away from this awful hour.

The doors burst open. She gripped Georgi's hand harder and tripped outside. Anya saw herself running in the silver chrome of a motorbike. Another high pitch, and then a blast ripped their fingers apart. They lifted off the pavement. Flying. Hurtling into shards of glass. *The glass will pierce my eyeballs. Or my heart. Is this what death tastes like?*

An arm, a foot, a head tore by. *Did I see a face? Or was that a ghost?* Anya couldn't expand her lungs. The air smelled metallic and her tongue burned like the end of a smoking gun. She retched on the chest of a large man lying over her legs. Blood gushed from the man's hip socket. *Where is his leg?*

Anya closed her eyes. Red and blue stars, then black. One second. One week. *Dead?* Her stomach rumbled.

sixteen

The air was one big scream. Anya opened her eyes. Chunks of skin, burnt hair, and blood covered Anya's capris and blouse. She scrunched her eyes closed. *Is this the road to Heaven? Or Hell?*

"Ahnnnnn-ya?" A lazy voice. *My name?* Georgi's voice wrapped her like a cocoon. She flexed her leg muscles, to stand up. She heard a chirp. *Go to Georgi. Where is my brother? Broken in two. I will never forgive myself.*

Pushing. She struggled to move the dead man. Three times. Wu wei, *push with the river.* Then she rolled out from under. She unfolded. Her muscles cramping. No cuts.

"Oh no. Help me!" Georgi cried. "Where are you? Anya! Anya!"

Anya wiped her face with a torn piece of shirt from the ground and pushed toward her brother's voice.

On the ground, leaning against a little boy. A body. Georgi struggled to stand but crumpled and fell forward. Anya put her ear to his chest and listened for his heartbeat. *Thump, thump, thump* like a greyhound race.

"I can't lift my arm. My elbow is ripped." His eyelids were swollen and his right arm was hanging at an odd angle. "I can't walk on this foot. I want Mama," Georgi cried. His eyelashes were gone. Her eyes stung with smoke and fear. People carrying the wounded over shoulders and hunched backs. *No one sees me. I am on my own.* She knelt like a donkey and motioned for Georgi to climb on. She fell flat, struggling under his weight, counted to three, and stood up. She sucked in a breath, and pushed a path through moaning people.

A deep crater had gouged the center of the crosswalk. A Sikh policeman lay motionless as a scarecrow, still pointing as if to guide the oncoming traffic. His eyes were open. His mustache was smoking.

"Oh my God," she said, and it rang out in the melody of the Kaddish. She stepped over limp bodies. A river of blood flowed around her feet. Wu wei, *go with the river.* A man inched on his stomach like a worm toward the alley. Snaking across the tar, an electrical cable sparking. A Red Cross truck screeched, stopped, turned off the siren.

"Help me. Help my brother, please. His arm!" She growled the plea to three Red Cross workers. Georgi's body shook like gelatin. "I will drop him if someone doesn't help me."

"Move to the end of the queue, miss. Life-threatening wounds and burns are treated first." The line stretched for a block or more. *I can't carry him there. I can't put him down on the tar. What if his arm falls off?* Georgi's tears wet her neck. She staggered. A burning tire rolled into her leg. When she fell, a man lifted Georgi off her. He swiped at the wet streams on her face with gauze and shone a light into her eyes.

"Don't move your head. Where do you hurt?"

"Check my brother, please," she pleaded.

The medic straightened and rotated Anya's arms.

"My brother is hurt. Not me."

"Your head is covered with blood. But not *your* blood, thank goodness." The medic took her hand and led her to a cot. He situated Georgi on her lap. Then he whipped around to the next cot and inspected an old man's thigh.

He cleaned and stitched and Anya's eyes followed the tip of the needle, in and out, in and out. Drops of sweat trailed from his forehead, dripping onto the steaming pavement. Six more steady stitches and he cut the black thread with his teeth.

"Splint, here," he instructed the Red Cross worker assisting him.

How does he stay as calm as a monk? "Georgi, we're safe," Anya said, shaking him. "Georgi? Open your eyes, little Joji."

She yelled to the medic, "Why won't he speak? Is he in a coma?"

"Most likely he's in shock." He pointed to the bone breaking through the skin of Georgi's lower arm. "A compound fracture."

Anya searched his face. The concern in his eyes revealed this was very bad news.

"The bones won't mend, and there's a risk of infection and then gangrene sets in," he explained. "If we take him to the Chinese hospital, they will amputate."

"Amputate?" Georgi's eyes popped open. He recoiled into the cot and the color drained from his cheeks.

Wu wei, *go with the river.*

An old woman collapsed on the pavement near Anya's feet, a fountain of blood spurting from her lower leg. The medic wrapped his hands around the woman's thigh above the knee, and squeezed hard.

Anya rubbed Georgi's temples in small circles. She kissed his hair and prayed to both of her Shabbat angels. *Save my brother's arm. He doesn't deserve to be hurt. And don't let another person in this world die.*

The medic grabbed Anya's hands and wrapped them where his had just been. "Squeeze hard until the bleeding stops. If the bandages soak through in less than thirty seconds, use a tourniquet."

"I'm not a doctor!"

The medic jumped over to a wounded man whose chest was impaled with a piece of wood.

What do I do? Her hands were shaking. Aunt Paulina would push up her sleeves, and help. So would Amelia Earhart.

Her heartbeat slowed. The grip in her fingers slowly steadied.

"So much blood," Georgi screamed.

"You're doing just fine." The medic called over the noise to her.

Trucks whizzed by. Magpies cawed. The woman groaned and closed her eyes. Wu wei, *the river.*

Anya calculated she'd applied pressure for less than fifteen seconds. Or was it fifteen minutes? All sound disappeared, except for her thumping heartbeat. She searched her memory for the page about tourniquets in Aunt Paulina's handbook. She pulled a large metal box marked with a red cross toward her and rifled through the bandages, syringes, pill bottles, vials, and medical instruments. No tourniquet.

She unwrapped her neck cloth. It was several inches too short. *Fashion a tourniquet from a strap, rope, string, or wire. Tie it with a square knot above, but as close as possible to the injury.* She tore the leather strap from her camera case, placed it over the cloth so she wouldn't pinch the woman's skin, and wrapped it around the wound, and tightened it. She tied a half knot. The knot slipped. *Shah!* The knot slipped again. Her third try, the knot stayed in place. She found a chopstick on the ground, and tied a square knot over it with the strap.

She twisted the stick until the tourniquet was tight and the bright red blood finally stopped flowing.

A nurse checked her work and nodded. "Loop the ends of the strap over the ends of—what is this? *Quai-tse?* Very smart thinking—then wrap it here above the knee so the chopstick won't loosen."

The nurse moved on to the next patient, a teenage girl. She called over her shoulder to Anya, "Mark her forehead with a *T* and write the time."

Anya dug though the box again. No writing implements. She didn't carry a pencil in her camera case. She could use lipstick. She'd borrowed one of Mama's enameled tubes— oxblood—from her vanity. She found it, threw the cap on the ground, and turned the gilt bottom. With the pointed tip, she wrote 2:59, and to be thorough, the military time—14:59—on the patient's forehead.

By the time another Red Cross truck pulled up, the old lady's cheeks had pinked up like a camellia petal. As the medic lifted her onto his stretcher, the woman nodded her head at Anya. Big Ching chimed three.

Anya spun around to tell the medic the good news. He was bending over a girl with lifeless eyes, a few cots away. His shoulders slumped, and he pushed her eyelids down with his middle finger, and covered her charred, blood-streaked face with a green military blanket.

Is she halfway between two worlds? Anya wondered.

"Anya! Anush. Thanks God, I found you!" It was Dedushka. He was running, clutching his side. He scrambled over the medical bag and wrapped Anya in his arms. His shirt was soaked with sweat and he was shivering.

"Dedushka!" Georgi cried. "My bones are broke."

"Are you related to the boy?" the medic asked Dedushka.

"Thank you for helping my grandchildren." Dedushka reached to shake his hand. "Chaim Orjich."

"Mr. Orjich, we are transporting your grandson to the Battle Creek Hospital. The care is unsurpassed in Shanghai. They have the most modern facilities. Maybe they can save his arm."

"I'm going in the Red Cross truck with my brother," Anya shouted.

Dedushka pushed his finger against his lips. "No, Anushkina, Chen is parked on the corner. Papa is out there somewhere." He swept his arm across the air. "Looking for you. He doesn't know Georgi is with you. Nor does your mama. You must go home. Your mama is waiting on pins and needles."

"*I* will accompany my grandson," he said, and pushed Anya to her feet. "Hurry, Anush. Stay close to the buildings."

"But I—"

"Anya. No more questions. Do as I say. Go to your mama."

He shook Anya's shoulders. "Anushkina, go now for the sake of God."

Go with the river. Wu wei.

seventeen

Someone had locked the front door. Anya pounded hard, then kicked the door with the heel of her sandal. Knocked and pounded.

How am I going to tell Mama?

Before Anya removed her finger from the mezusah, the front door flew open and Mama's arms wrapped around her, so tight it was hard to breath. Mama rocked her and kissed both cheeks.

"Oh my God. Blood everywhere. Your shirt"—again she kissed both cheeks—"your legs"—kissed her forehead, the tip of her nose—"you are covered with blood"—kissed both eyelids. She patted Anya's collarbone and waist, and dropped to her knees to inspect Anya's toes.

Anya cried for the first time today. Mama's fingers were covered with blood.

"I was sick with worry," Mama whispered, and kissed Anya's big toe. "When I got up from my nap, you weren't in your room. But your birds were. And the Benatars were gone."

She stood and closed her eyes. Her lips moved silently.

"It's okay, Mama. I'm here. I'm not hurt, not even a scratch."

"We heard a report that planes bombed the Palace Hotel and the Great World Gambling Heaven—"

"—not gambling heaven, Mama, Amusement Palace," Anya said.

"Papa and Dedushka ordered Chen to start the car. Can you imagine? Papa in a car on Shabbat? Between his duty to save his children and his duties to God, he chose you. He was certain God didn't need his help. And the Palace Hotel. Oh my God! A bomb on the Bund. Thanks God my Georgi is sleeping *Shabbos* away in Dedushka's room like he always does."

She rang her bell and yelled, "Dandan. Wake up, Georgi. Tell him Anya is—"

"—Georgi isn't sleeping, Mama. I didn't obey Li Mei, and I hopped on the trolley to Siccawei. And Georgi had followed her. But she didn't know it. When the trolley started up, we discovered Georgi one seat back."

"Where is he?" Mama said. Her voice sounded breathless.

"It's all right, Mama. He's with Dedushka," Anya said carefully, choosing her words with great care as she did whenever she told a half truth. "Li Mei directed me to take Georgi home. Georgi begged me to let him ride the seesaw on the roof of—"

"Oh my God." Mama's hand went up and covered her mouth. "But you said he is safe."

"Mama. He's alive. He's with Dedushka and a medic."

"Why is Dedushka with a doctor? Did he have a heart attack—"

"MAMA. Nothing is wrong with Dedushka. It's Georgi. His arm is broken."

Mama shuddered and put a trembling hand to her throat.

"Badly broken, Mama. He's going to need surgery." Anya felt sick to her stomach.

Mama covered her ears and rushed away from the open door. Anya followed her to the parlor. Mama ran in a circle and crumpled on the rug.

My mama has fainted and all I can do is stand here like the Victory Angel.

"Where is my son?" Mama stopped sniffing. "We must go to him *immediatement*." She stood up. Her voice sounded like Mama B.C.

"A Red Cross truck transported Georgi and Dedushka to Battle Creek Sanitarium."

"   the White China man's hospital?" Mama swiped at her eyes.

"His name is Dr. Miller. I met him at Marco Polo Market yesterday when I was searching for goat's milk for Kisa. You thought I was taking my Shabbat bath—"

"Not the Jewish Hospital?"

"No, Mama."

"We must go to Georgi now. Anya, take me there. Where is Papa?"

"Probably still looking for me," Anya said, her forehead furrowed. "I'll tell Mo-chou where we're going so when he comes home she can send him there. Chen left the motor running. I'll get Babushka."

The doorbell rang and rang and rang. Someone was banging loudly and urgently on the front door. Mo-Chou answered. Running footsteps. Bustling in the foyer. Jia Li burst into the room, followed by Mo-chou.

"—big guns blew up Frenchtown, then planes flew over, Chinese planes, not Japanese devil planes. I thought I saw the god of the Ministry of Time in the International Settlement yesterday. His presence in one neighborhood means great injury is coming soon next door. Where is Li Mei?" Jia Li demanded.

She took one long look at Anya's face, and said, "Miss Ani-ah. What happened to my Li Mei?"

"You must have crossed paths with each other, and missed. Last I saw her, she was on the Siccawei trolley with a baby in a sling."

"No trolley. I ran here, all five miles. The trolleys are blocked by barricades." Jia Li collapsed in a chair. "What baby?"

"Li Mei will tell you later. We have to go. My Georgi was wounded in the explosion near Great World," Mama said. "Send Li Mei to Battle Creek Hospital when she returns." Mama paused then, tears welling in her eyes. "God willing, she will return, Jia Li."

*T*he hallway smelled like the color white, a sharp odor mixed with alcohol, soap, and peroxide. Rattling by, under the bright lights, was a cart with steel trays filled with cotton, gauze, vials, and needles. Sitting in the chairs were men and women cradling pain in their hands.

Two sets of loud purposeful footsteps made their way from the dim end of the hall: Dr. Miller's followed by Dedushka's.

"Georgi's break is a compound fracture," Dr. Miller said. "The ulna and radius shattered."

Dedushka put one arm around Mama's shoulder, the other around Babushka's. She had a faraway look like she hadn't heard a word. Mama nodded at the doctor.

"Because the bone ends are not in line with each other, they will not heal in the correct position. Georgi won't be able to use that arm. An infection, or worse, gangrene, could set in."

Anya imagined her brother no longer able to hold his BB gun, swing a bat, toss a ball. She turned her hand, palm up, palm down, palm up.

"The safest bet is to amputate unless . . ."

Mama cried out as though someone had smacked her face. It was a sharp scream from deep in her throat, followed by a sucking in of air. "I want to speak to a Jewish doctor. Oh my God, where is my husband? Why didn't we stay put in Odessa where we belong? This wouldn't have happened to my only son."

"Enough, young lady." Dedushka pointed a warning finger at his daughter. "Stella, do not insult the good doctor."

"Amen," Babushka whispered.

"My hospital is hosting Dr. Weatherby from Harvard Medical School. He developed a new surgical technique for these fractures. He is in Shanghai to train our doctors to save the limbs of wounded soldiers."

"I would like to speak to him, please," Mama said.

"Of course." Dr. Miller strode from the room.

The last time they sat together in a circle with long faces was in their living room in Odessa, minutes before they locked the front door for the last time and snuck into their cars for the silent ride to the train station.

Ten minutes passed before a tall, bald man wearing blue hospital scrubs entered the room, followed by Dr. Miller.

"I am game to operate on your son but the procedure is experimental and I don't pretend to have the right license to perform internal fixation surgery on civilians in Shanghai."

"We don't care about the license," Dedushka said.

"Are you qualified?" Babushka said.

"You may ask America's leader. I am one of President Roosevelt's consulting physicians."

"That's good enough for my brother," Anya said.

"Papachka, should I give my permission?" Mama asked.

Both of Anya's grandparents nodded their heads.

Dr. Weatherby led the family to a busy room where Georgi and half a dozen other patients lay on cots. Georgi's face was pallid. His eyes were half open but he appeared to be asleep.

"He never sleeps with his eyes open at home," Anya said.

"It's the trauma and the morphine. He's out of pain. When I explained that we will put him to sleep for the operation, he begged me to let him stay awake and watch. Brave boy!"

"He takes after his sister." Mama nodded. "Thank you, Anush."

This *Mama, I recognize.*

"Your son's surgery will take several hours, then we'll wheel him to the recovery room. You can wait or go home, then return."

"I am not stepping one foot outside the doors of this hospital until my boy is out of surgery," Mama said.

"A pregnant woman has no business sleeping in an armchair in a hospital!" Papa walked in the room with a determined stride.

"Papa!" Anya cried, and ran to hold Mama's hand.

"Rosen—Joshua!" Mama sighed, then sunk down on the cot next to Georgi.

While Georgi was in surgery, Papa reassured Mama about Dr. Miller. "He is revered in villages all over China. When he visits, the local magistrates give up their private sedan chairs for his supreme comfort. The townspeople line the road to greet him and offer sweets as though he were a king."

To kill some time, Dedushka suggested the ladies fulfill the mitzvah of *bikkur holim*, visiting the sick. It was easy to find the entrance to the crowded barracks-style military ward. Li T'ieh-kuai, also known as "Iron-crutch Li," carrying a crutch and a gourd, was posted over the door. He was the Immortal who brings comfort to those who are ill. Mama and Anya scurried through the room, cheering up the wounded soldiers. Babushka fed ice chips to the men whose lips were parched.

"Anya, help me prop up this boy!" Mama said.

They pushed three pillows behind the small of his back, then moved to the next soldier. His left leg was gone and the stump was wrapped in white gauze. Anya placed a rolled blanket under his right knee.

"Is that more comfortable?" she asked him.

He didn't answer. Anya began to hum the *Mishebarach*, the prayer for healing. "Mama, sing with me?"

When Mama got to the notes of the *refuah shleimah*, Anya harmonized with her for the wish for a speedy recovery. When they finished the song, a dozen or so soldiers and civilians clapped, and so did Babushka.

*M*ama suggested they get a cup of tea in the cafeteria. They were sipping from the chipped cups, when Mama cleared her throat. "You're old enough now for me to tell you this: Stella is not my real name."

Anya gulped her hot tea. "Mama?"

"My given name was Shulamit before I changed it to Stella for my singing career."

Anya fidgeted in the uncomfortable hard chair.

"I wanted to change my last name, too, to something musical, not identifiable as Russian or German sounding. But Dedushka wouldn't hear of it."

"Mama? I want to change my name, too." She intended to make her voice strong like Li Mei's but the words slipped out as weak as little pebbles skipping over the surface of a pond and as she cleared her throat to begin again, Papa ran into the cafeteria.

"I see nothing wrong with you taking a stage name, Anush," Mama said.

"I'm not talking about for the stage. I want a name of my own!"

Anya could no longer stop the words sitting on her tongue,

ready to roll out. "I know you have your heart set on me singing opera. But, Mama, when I sail to America and ride the train from San Francisco to New York . . . I plan to attend Columbia University, not Juilliard," Anya blurted, and waited for Mama to become agitated.

But Mama didn't. She looked calmly at Anya, stared directly into her eyes.

"After I earn my baccalaureate, I plan to go to Columbia Medical School. Amelia Earhart went there, too, but she didn't stick it out to become a doctor. That's what I want to do with my life, be a doctor. Like Aunt Paulina."

No more hidden wishes. I finally told Mama my dream. No one can argue with the truth.

"Papa! Over here." Anya waved at him.

"Have you announced your plans to Maestro?" Mama asked.

"Of course not. I wanted to tell you first."

Mama searched Papa's smiling face. "Georgi is still in surgery but Dr. Weatherby sent a resident out to tell us the operation was successful and he is suturing the incision."

"Mazel tov." Mama and Anya clapped.

I risked Mama's reaction. I can deal with whatever comes next.

"Ya lu blue ti biah," Mama said.

"I love you, too, Mama," Anya said.

eighteen

While Mama and Papa waited for Georgi to wake up in the recovery room, Anya asked a nurse for help. In no time, she had collected two half-burnt candles from the hospital chapel, a tin of grape juice, a tea sachet, and an empty bedpan she made sure had been sterilized—makeshift ritual objects necessary for their Havdalah service tonight. The nurse also showed her the perfect spot to gather together outside.

When it was dark, Anya led Mama, Papa, Dedushka, and Babushka—the Rosen family minus Georgi—outdoors to the koi pond in the Battle Creek garden.

"Anushkina, look," Mama said, pointing at the first twinkling star. The five of them moved into a circle with their shoulders grazing.

"I bet I can find the second star before you," Papa said.

Anya squealed, "There's the second one *and* the third. I am the queen of the skies."

The appearance of the three twinkling stars marked the distinct moment between the end of Shabbat and the other six days of the week. *"La-y'hudim hay'ta ora v'simha v'sason vikar, ken tih'yeh lanu,"* Dedushka chanted. There is light and joy, gladness and honor for the Jewish people. So may we be blessed.

The waning moon, just a bit less full than last night, reflected in Mama's eyes. Her forehead was smooth. Papa poured the juice into the bedpan. *"Barukh ata Adonai Eloheinu melekh ha-olam bo-re p'ri hagafen."* Blessed is the Lord our God, Ruler of the Universe, Creator of the fruit of the vine.

A shadow moved from the corner.

Is that a hungry ghost? Did a spirit fly from the skies to steal Georgi's soul? As the ghost sprinted toward the circle, the candlelight and moonbeams revealed its face. Instead of a black hole, Anya saw Li Mei, beaming.

"Don't worry, Madame," she said, "I checked *Huang Li,* the Imperial Calendar we use to pick lucky dates for weddings, business deals, funerals. Today is an auspicious day for Georgi's surgery."

"Don't say 'funeral,'" Babushka said in her warning tone. "It is unnatural for a mother, or a babushka, to bury a child."

"Mamochka, don't be morbid," Mama said.

Li Mei sidled next to Anya and whispered in her ear, "Jules helped me pass through the barricades. Mah-mee told me where to find you." Anya took the cook's hand in hers and squeezed it gently, grateful to see Li Mei was safe.

Papa nodded at Li Mei and passed the bedpan to Dedushka, "This is the Havadalah cup—"

"—God forbid," Dedushka said, but took a long sip of grape juice. "This is the cup that Jews have raised for thousands of years on Saturday night to mark the end of the joyful day of rest, and to toast the holiness of being alive. May the One who separates the sacred and profane make us secure and as numerous as grains of sand and the stars in the night."

Warmed by the wine, Shabbat passed over to the days of the active week.

Anya couldn't wait for the ceremony to end to ask Li Mei about Kisa. "Did you meet Kisa's mother? How is the baby? When can I go to Siccawei?"

"Kisa is fine. Mo Li, her mother, was so happy to see her baby again. After hearing the story of your compassion, Mo Li named the baby in your honor."

Anya began to cry quietly.

"Her name is Lin-lin, which means 'beauty of a tinkling bell.'"

Anya's flow of tears was like a river going its own way, in celebration, and in sorrow. For little girls who aren't wanted, and for those who are precious. For Nazis taking life from the Jews. For mothers giving life to babies. Anya cried for how difficult Kisa's and Mo Li's next few years were likely to be, and she cried for Mama's disappointment.

And she cried for joy.

Papa reached for her hand. He didn't ask her to stop, even though they hadn't completed Havdalah. He gave her the two candle stubs, which would serve as the traditional braided candle with two wicks to symbolize the intertwining of their family with the Jewish people, and all people, around the world.

Anya offered one stub to Li Mei and they lit both. Dedushka, Papa, Babushka, and Mama waved their hands in front of the candles with palms facing their bodies. The glow of the fire played with the pink shadows in their fingernails.

Anya sensed her *neshamah yeteira* fly away. But she didn't feel alone, or lonely, without her second soul because Mama was standing by her side, carrying a baby in her womb—maybe another little girl—who would never sleep anywhere but in a warm cradle.

Mama smelled the cinnamon and clove tea sachet. Then she walked around the inside of the circle, passing the little silk bag under the noses of her family. The aroma worked to mark the end of the old week and the beginning of the new. And to remind the Rosens of miracles.

Wake up, Anya. It's a new week. May it be a good week, a week of peace.

Papa said the prayer affirming the Creator of the spice, then Dedushka chanted the final prayer of Havdalah, which distinguishes between the seventh day of rest—Shabbat—and the other six days of the week.

Anya and Li Mei doused the flames in the wine puddled at the bottom of the bedpan.

We are different and we are the same.

Mama's voice sang out, "*Shavua tov, Shavua tov, Shavua tov, Shavua tov*, a good week, a week of peace, may gladness reign and joy increase."

Many stars twinkled in the summer sky waiting for the constellations to appear and for Shabbat to come to an end.

Shavua tov.

The family stopped at Georgi's bed to kiss him good night. Mama pulled the crisp sheet and soft blue blanket tight

179

to remove the wrinkles and tucked the edges of the bedding around Georgi's ears. He didn't open his eyes. His head lay still in the deep indent of the pillow.

Li Mei dug out of her pocket a small tin of Buddha balm and rubbed a dab on his temples. She spoke to him as if he could hear her bedtime story through his dreams.

"Remember brave Guan-Gong, the peaceful deity, the Eighth Immortal? Many centuries ago, his arm was badly damaged during battle. Secret potions and salves couldn't heal him. The only cure was surgery. He was so brave that, while the field surgeons pulled his tendons into place and sewed him up with a needle and thread, he played a game of solitaire with his good hand."

Papa listened and didn't scold Li Mei for telling tall tales.

How will I sleep tonight without the sound of Georgi snoring on the other side of the wall?

When they exited the hospital, Chen was waiting for them with the car motor running. He had news about why the Chinese had devastated their own city. Shrapnel from Japanese antiaircraft guns had damaged the bomb racks of the two Chinese fighter planes. Fearing their bombs might fall on the city, the pilots intended to navigate to an open field. But one bomb exploded prematurely at the Palace Hotel and the other two on Boulevard Edward VII outside Great World Amusement Palace. "Bloody Saturday" was a terrible and unfortunate accident.

He drove as quickly as possible through the crowded streets of Frenchtown. Windows were boarded up and sandbags piled the entrances of Jardin & Matheson, the Shanghai Club, the British Consulate General, and the other large buildings. Anya turned her eyes away from the hordes of coolies pushing squeaky wheelbarrows once she realized they were piled with bodies. She wanted to scream but instead plugged her nose and buried her face in Dedushka's chest.

At the top of the Rosens' driveway, Chen stopped the car and jumped out to help Mama and Babushka exit from the front seat. Anya and Papa escorted Dedushka to the front door.

Li Mei called out to Anya, "Someone is here to see you, Miss Ani-ah," and she darted around the trellis, and headed to the kitchen door.

The lamp-lit rickshaw was parked in the turnaround.

"I've been waiting for over an hour!" Bobby shouted from the glowing cab.

"We were at the hospital waiting for Georgi to come through surgery. He broke his arm in the bombing," Anya said.

"Those chink pilots couldn't control their own damn planes. My father says no wonder the Japanese are taking over China without much of a struggle," Bobby said.

Bobby's driver Xi bowed to Anya and wouldn't look in her eyes.

She understood the true meaning of "coolie," which Li Mei had once explained means "bitter strength." Bobby's remark reminded Anya of Natalie Samson's demeaning names for the Chinese, the Japanese, the Poles, and the Jews.

Gabriel Benatar would never call a person by anything but a proper name.

"Georgi's alive but he almost lost his arm!" Anya added.

Bobby didn't appear to hear her. He retrieved an envelope from his seat pocket and held it out to Anya. "I stole the last invitation from my mother's drawer." He pulled himself up tall.

"If you want me to read it, then please get out of the rickshaw and give it to me," Anya said.

Bobby hopped down from his seat reluctantly, without help from Xi. He grabbed Anya's hand and wrapped her fingers around the embossed seal on the flap. "No more strikes against us," Bobby joked.

Anya scanned the perfectly formed calligraphed letters, all the details about Bobby's bowling party on Tuesday. She couldn't think of anything to say.

I don't want to stand outside in the hot, smelly night with Bobby Sassoon.

A round of gun shots sounded from the direction of Soochow Creek. Anya jumped and had the urge to cover her head. But it wasn't fear that kept her from speaking. She had believed that lovesickness caused her to clam up around Bobby.

It isn't my tongue that is clumsy; the problem isn't mine. My silence has nothing to do with love.

Bobby grabbed her hand. He seemed disturbed, quizzically searching her mouth for a smile. When Anya didn't give him the reaction he expected, he kissed her middle knuckle and said, "See you at the party of the year!"

Bobby Sassoon is so selfish—like Narcissus who only had eyes for his own reflection—that he doesn't care one bit about anyone else's feelings.

Anya shook her head. "Send your mother my regrets. I volunteer at the hospital on Tuesdays cheering up brave Chinese soldiers."

"Too bad for you. Everyone is coming."

Bobby jumped in the cab of his rickshaw and settled back

into the velvet pillows. Xi bent over and groaned as he lifted the brass handles. The rickshaw pulled away and the last thing Anya saw of Bobby was his hand batting mosquitoes away from his face.

*A*nya touched her fingertips to her lips and then the mezuzah and ran straight upstairs to Georgi's room. She gathered a couple of comic books and his tin truck with the wind-up crane to bring to her brother tomorrow. She found his radio in the fort under his bed but waited until she closed the door to her room to turn up the volume. It was time for the BBC report from London, hopefully with news of Amelia Earhart.

Writing about her eventful Shabbat in her *Book of Moons* could wait until later. She sat down on the vanity bench and stared at herself in the mirror while rubbing pomade on her curls. *Bad habit, I know. That's why they call it a vanity.*

Someone new was looking out. Her face had changed. She seemed more colorful and sparkling, and bright as the moon.

Anya opened the door to the terrace, hoping that Giselle wouldn't jump out from behind the bamboo tonight. She was tired and wanted to wait until the morning to tell her friend about Georgi and Kisa. And Gabriel. And Mama. Tomorrow they'd meet in Little Vienna for a linzer torte and she'd fill her in.

Out in the river, a sampan lit by swinging lamps had dropped anchor. Anya counted eight people washing themselves and their laundry in the river water.

How do they bear no privacy, no space to call their own in a one-room boat?

At least they had a home. The family camped at her driveway this morning didn't. Nor did the thousands of refugees streaming into Shanghai from the villages. Nor the Jews who arrived every month from Europe with one suitcase each, wearing the keys to their front doors on strings around their necks, in case one day they were lucky enough to go home.

She wondered if Amelia Earhart had brought her house key with her on the Electra. And if she had, was she clutching it for courage in the moonlight? Or was the key lost in the sand at the bottom of the ocean where light from the sun and the moon couldn't reach it?

Anya leaned over the railing farther than was safe. Mrs. Lindberg wasn't standing at her easel but the lamp was lit. She was probably tucking in the younger children and when it was her time to be alone would paint long into the night.

Anya called out to the side of Giselle's house a short message to herself, emphasizing the first three words.

Clear as a bell, "I see you, Moon" echoed through the courtyard. She inhaled the strong perfume of the garden and a waft of the river and wondered if Kisa was awake, too.

author's note

As a teenager, I listened to the exotic, terrifying, and comical accounts of my Jewish father's childhood in the French Quarter of Shanghai, China. My grandfather, Issai Abramovitch, formerly a high-ranking government official in Odessa, Russia (now Ukraine), had refused to join the Communist Party, a decision that provoked a death threat. He packed up his family and they fled to Shanghai, a safe haven to which many Jewish families escaped religious persecution. Issai parlayed his writing skills into a career as a journalist. My grandmother, Asya, a classically trained opera singer, joined the local amateur opera company and juggled motherhood, hat making, and performing.

When my father, Yan Abramovitch, was eight years old, he found a Chinese baby girl abandoned on a curb and carried her home. Issai and Asya, afraid of contracting cholera, called the sanitation department and the baby was removed. It was at this heartbreaking passage in Yan's life that he decided to become a doctor and save lives. He sailed to America by himself at seventeen, attended the University of California at Los Angeles, then Stanford Medical School. For forty-eight years, he cared for San Francisco's children. He was the only Jewish physician in the city who spoke Mandarin and Russian, as well as English and French, fluently. Consequently, he provided pediatric care to thousands of Asian families as well as the families of the Russian consulate. As an "old school" doctor, he made house calls, worked seven days a week, and handed out free infant formula to the needy until his death at age seventy-five in 2004.

His sister, Lily, attended French schools and mastered four languages, in preparation for life in America and its golden opportunities. She applied to and was accepted at Juilliard School of Music in New York City, but transferred after one year to paid employment as a secretary at the United Nations. She met Sergeant Bernard Gross, married, and became mother to two boys, but never stopped singing. Her antique console piano was handed down to my daughter, Lily, who composes songs at the keyboard.

In 1937, four thousand Jews lived in Frenchtown, soon to become a "solitary island" in the midst of Japanese-occupied China. Their ranks swelled to twenty thousand with the influx of Eastern European Jews escaping Hitler's march across Europe. As doors closed all over the world to desperate families, Shanghai customs officials did not require a visa to enter the city. But soon, the Japanese herded the refugees into the Hongkew Ghetto for the remainder of World War II. My family, and other Russian Jews who had arrived before 1937, were fortunate; the occupiers allowed them to remain in their comfortable homes. They snuck food, reading material, clothing, and blankets into the ghetto, bringing small comforts and subsistence to the Jews who fled the Nazis. This is a little-known chapter of Jewish Holocaust history.

By war's end, with the impending advancement of the Communist Party, the Shanghai Jews packed up their lives, leaving no marker of the places they'd lived in, no trace of who they were. My aunt and father booked passage on ships bound for the United States in 1946 and 1947, respectively. My grandparents had divorced in 1936 and the same day my grandmother married Zelik Zelikovsy, a lawyer and partner in an import/export business. Issai died of a stroke in 1950, alone on a beach in Formosa. His body was transported back to Shanghai and buried in the Jewish Cemetery next to his father-in-law, Israel Orjich, who died in 1930.

The United States rejected Asya and Zelik's application for permission to immigrate so they sailed to Paris in 1952. After numerous petitions to Congress, they reunited in 1955 with Yan and Lily in New York.

During the Cultural Revolution in 1967, protesters razed the four Jewish cemeteries and scattered the marble tombstones throughout villages on the outskirts of Shanghai. The people used them as washing stones and for bridging shallow creeks. In 2003, an Israeli journalist discovered "Dedushka's" cracked tombstone leaning against a hut in Minzhu 6 village. The relocation project workers have since gathered eighty markers and are drafting plans to construct either a New Jewish Cemetery of Shanghai (possibly in a section of the Shanghai Buddhist Cemetery) or an exhibition in the inner yard of Ohel Moshe, the ghetto synagogue, now a Jewish museum. While vandals continue to assault Jewish cemeteries throughout Europe, the Chinese people guard the tombstones with respect and reverence.

To see a photo of Israel Orjich's tombstone, visit the web site: www.shanghaijewishmemorial.com. Click "Arzich, Israel."

Anya's War portrays historical people and actual events, although the book is a work of fiction. I created the majority of the characters—their actions, dialogue, and musings—in my imagination; however, the settings, historical events, and cultural beliefs are those of twentieth-century Odessa and Shanghai.

Peace and shalom,
Andrea Alban

The real Anya in Shanghai, circa 1938

Thank you for reading this
FEIWEL AND FRIENDS book.
The Friends who made

Anya's War

possible are:

Jean Feiwel, publisher

Liz Szabla, editor-in-chief

Rich Deas, creative director

Elizabeth Fithian, marketing director

Holly West, assistant to the publisher

Dave Barrett, managing editor

Nicole Liebowitz Moulaison,
production manager

Anna Roberto, editorial assistant

Ksenia Winnicki, publishing associate

Elizabeth Tardiff, designer

Find out more about our authors and
artists and our future publishing at
www.feiwelandfriends.com.

OUR BOOKS ARE
FRIENDS FOR LIFE